Chloe

Chloe

Joe "Bondi" Beach

CLEARING RAIN PRESS
SAN FRANCISCO, CALIFORNIA
clearing.rain.press@gmail.com

CHLOE

ISBN: 978-1-365-30750-8

18 17 16   1 2 3

This book is a work of fiction. Names, characters, places, and incidents are the product of the author's imagination or are used fictitiously. Any resemblance to actual events or persons, living or dead, is entirely coincidental.

Portions of this work were published separately as "Pink Undies: Chloe at Thanksgiving" (2010); "Fire and Ice: Chloe at Christmas" (2010); and "Pagan Spring: Chloe at Easter" (2013); as well as together in a digital edition, "Chloe" (2014).

Second Edition (Print)

PRINTED IN THE UNITED STATES OF AMERICA

T

Acknowledgments

The cover image and frontispiece is *Naket i Eldsken* ("Nude in Firelight"), 1904, by Anders Zorn. It is in the public domain in the United States.

Chloe

"We will exult and rejoice in you ..."
— from *Song of Solomon*, NSRV

I look at my daughter and see myself reflected in her face.
My bones, my flesh and blood run through her.

— from "My Beautiful College Girl," by Lydia Dillingham

1 Thanksgiving

"YES YES YES YES, oh god oh god don't stop don't stop!"

I had Kathleen's legs back against her shoulders. No way I was stopping.

"Yeah yeah yeah!"

In the next moment, though, I throbbed and spurted as deep inside her as I could get and I had to stop then.

"Oh, god."

"You can say that again."

She smiled up at me, her lips soft and a little puffy, her eyes dreamy.

"Oh, god."

"Hah hah hah."

I softened and slipped out and moved off her. She turned into my arms and kissed me.

"So, you liked that picture, huh?"

"What's the deal, Kathleen?"

She laughed.

"The deal is, John, we have a very cute daughter."

No kidding, I was thinking. Slim but curvy in the right places, just like her mother. Her mother's grey eyes. Sexy in a swimsuit, too, like that was a surprise. But in her underwear?

"OK. And?"

"I mean, she's probably tearing up her freshman dorm and breaking hearts left and right even as we speak."

I looked at my spouse.

"How about you start with who took the picture? I want to have a few words with him, especially if it was one of her creep high school classmates."

Most of Chloe's friends were normal-looking, whatever that means these days, but then there was that kid with a ring through his nose and a ponytail, and he wasn't the only weird one. Not my type at all, until Chloe told us he'd been on the honors list every semester since middle school and was in line to be valedictorian. That didn't make him look any better to me, really, but I figured at least he probably wasn't a total stoner.

A giggle.

"A few words with her, actually."

"Huh?"

"I took the picture, silly."

"When? Where?"

"In Florida. Don't you remember? Chloe came down to Orlando at the end of my conference in February. We went to Disney World and we did a little shopping, too."

"Yeah?"

Kathleen put her lips right against my ear and her hand on my cock.

"It was her idea. Chloe picked them out. She said dusky rose was your favorite color."

Boy, the kid got that right. It's not as though the bra and panties were all that revealing, but her smooth skin and the color packed a wallop. Did Chloe know her mother was wearing dusky rose on our honeymoon? I started to stiffen again and I thrust against Kathleen's palm without thinking.

"I can tell you like that idea, right? That she knew what color you like?"

Like it? Is she crazy? I was practically ready to come again just hearing Kathleen tell me the story. I mean, this isn't the first time I'd gotten a hard-on thinking about Chloe. Never done anything about it, although there's been more than once when I've found it necessary to jump Kathleen's bones after watching Chloe in her bikini at the pool, or on a Saturday morning in t-shirt and panties. I wasn't sure Kathleen had noticed.

"Kathleen?"

"You heard me."

"You mean she wanted to do this, right?"

"Yes."

Kathleen paused.

"You know something else? I know you've been watching her."

She rubbed her palm flat against me. I shoved back.

"You think I don't know why you jumped me those times?"

She curled her fingers around my cock and began stroking.

"And another thing?"

Her hand was moving a little faster now.

"Chloe knows you were watching her and she liked it."

I was getting close.

"What's more? I liked being jumped. Especially then."

I erupted into her hand. Kathleen released me when I finished and grabbed my t-shirt to clean me and her hand. Just as she finished I heard something between a snicker and a giggle.

"Would it disappoint you, John, to know that's a bathing suit Chloe is wearing, not underwear?"

I thought about it for about two seconds.

"No."

She leaned over to take me in her mouth for a moment before she moved up to kiss me, slowly and thoroughly.

"Good."

A couple of weeks later I came back to the question I'd been mulling.

"So, tell me about Chloe. How do you know what she wants?"

Kathleen kind of runs things in our household, and there's a reason for that. The Gulf War, the first one, was enough to convince me the Army wasn't going to be my calling, even if I learned some interesting skills.

I write about some of it. I might not be Tim O'Brien, but I'm not too bad. People pay me for my stuff. I love writing, Kathleen knew it, so she proposed the terms early in our marriage.

"John, you write and run things at home and I'll take care of everything else, OK?"

That sounded pretty good to me and that's the way it's been. My stuff gets published here and there, mostly short fiction. I've got a novel in my head but not much on paper yet.

Of course, "everything else" wasn't really true. Kathleen supported us, yes, and I was at home writing, but that's only part of the story. I wrote on my own schedule pretty much, but there was all that other stuff that goes with running the home. The best part? That's easy. It was all the time I got to spend with Chloe when she was little.

At first I got some funny looks from the husbands of our neighbors and the parents of Chloe's classmates, but when they realized I wasn't on the make for their wives or their kids we all got along. I think there might have been a disappointed wife or two when the women found out I wasn't interested, although I'm probably overestimating myself.

It took a little while, but eventually they all realized I was a dad at home and the designated parent for our family at school events, not a loser who liked to hang around children and their mommies.

A couple of years ago Kathleen declined a partnership offer

at her firm. When you make partner you get saddled with more schmoozing, much of it at night, and none of us wanted that. Instead, she took a salary cap in exchange for limited hours and a pretty stable track as a senior associate. Kathleen's decision suited Chloe and me just fine. We were comfortable financially, and Chloe and I got to see more of Kathleen this way.

So, yeah, Chloe and I got along fine. In fact, we'd sort of grown up together, you could say, but I was coming to realize Chloe and Kathleen communicated in a way I'd never understand.

"Hey, where are you?"

Kathleen poked me.

I shook my head. Admired Kathleen's curves and smooth skin in the afternoon sun beside our pool. Late October, one sun-filled Indian summer day after another. Perfect for swimming and sunning. We were alone, no need for swimsuits.

"Thinking about Chloe."

"Remember last August, just before she left for college? We were all out here together?"

I remembered.

"Chloe and I took our tops off. Remember that?"

Oh boy, did I. They were on their tummies so I couldn't see much, but their bareness and tiny bikinis meant were an arousing treat, anyway.

Another poke.

"Hey, pal. Are you with me here?"

I shook my head again, trying to clear it.

"Sort of. I guess. Yeah, I remember."

Kathleen shook her own head, but she put her hand on my thigh. That felt good.

"Anyway, it's not as though you could see anything, right?"

"No."

"Chloe asked me what was up with you, although I think

she knew. 'One word,' I said to her. 'Boobs.' You know what she did then?"

I shook my head once more.

"She lifted up a little and turned on her side to face me. 'Like these, you mean?'

"I was speechless."

Kathleen's hand on my thigh moved a little higher.

"I asked her what the heck she thought she was doing."

Kathleen's gentle fingers cradled my balls.

" 'Just this, Mom,' she answered. And she leaned over and kissed me, a light kiss, on the lips.

"John, I have to tell you that once again I didn't know what to say. I looked at Chloe for the longest time. She didn't move. Looked back at me with that Zen look she has, you know the one? Where you can't tell what she's thinking? That little minx. She knew exactly what she was doing.

"And you know what else? Maybe I hadn't known what was going on but now I was getting a pretty good idea fast. What's more, I realized right then I wasn't as upset as I thought I'd be. I mean, I didn't know what to think, but you get what I'm saying, right?

"In fact, it was a little bit the opposite of upset, you know?"

I hadn't known, but I was starting to get the picture myself. I was rigid, and Kathleen moved her hand from my balls and began stroking me. She paused, leaned over a little more and kissed me, her lips parted, her tongue offering a challenge to mine. It was a quick battle, over practically before it started, and Kathleen backed off and resumed her story.

"After a moment, I glanced down and saw her nipples were erect. She saw me looking and grinned as she looked back at my breasts. My nipples were as hard as hers.

" 'You OK, Mom?' She was still grinning. I was starting to smile a little myself. I leaned forward and gave her a quick kiss. 'Time to cover up, Chloe. Your dad will be back in a few minutes.'

"Her grin got wider. 'Maybe next time I'll wait for him.' She kissed me again, not so lightly this time, jumped up, gave me a little wave and walked back inside, wrapping herself in her towel as she went. A minute later you came out of the house looking, I have to say, kind of stunned."

That's because Chloe had let her towel slip when she passed me in the living room. She had winked, too.

I started to tell Kathleen this but it was too late. Kathleen leaned over into my lap and her tongue was wet and warm and it couldn't have been more than a minute before I spurted. She swallowed it all and licked up a little bit at the corner of her mouth. I watched Kathleen take a swig of her beer and spit it out. She smiled, and I think I heard her giggle.

"She has really nice boobs, too."

As if I didn't know.

Chloe called when Kathleen and I were just finishing dinner Sunday evening in the first week of November.

"Hi Dad!"

"Hi Chloe, how are you?"

"Good!"

"What's new?"

If you've ever had a kid at college you probably know how these conversations go—a little about last week's paper and she stayed up really late, a roommate story or two, how bad the food is, blah blah blah. Never anything about how drunk she got on Saturday night, funny about that. There are some things you probably don't want to know about, anyway. We got through the pleasantries pretty quickly.

"So, Dad, did Mom show you anything?"

What the hell? I won't pretend I didn't know what she was talking about, but I still had no idea what to say. "You looked so hot I wanted to eat you up," didn't sound right, even if it was true.

"Um."

"Dad, the photo?"

"Yeah, sweetie, she did."

"Did you like it?"

"You looked really cute, Chloe."

"Did you like the color, Dad?"

"You know I did."

She giggled.

"Good!"

"Sweetie, I think I'd better put your mom on the phone. Here she is."

Kathleen grabbed the phone and made a shooing motion with her hand. I stayed out of the kitchen and I couldn't quite hear Kathleen's end of the conversation, but there seemed to be a lot of giggling and laughter. Then Kathleen raised her voice.

"OK, Chloe. Go ahead and send them. I think you know he'll like them."

Kathleen came to sit beside me in front of the fire, but she wouldn't tell me what that was about.

"John!"

"Yeah?"

"Come here."

I finished loading the dishwasher and walked into our den office where Kathleen sat in front of our main machine a couple of days after Chloe's telephone call.

"What's up?"

"Chloe sent us some pictures."

I felt a little flutter. After my conversation with Chloe on Sunday, and listening to Kathleen and Chloe giggle and conspire on the phone, I knew something was going on.

Kathleen opened the attachments. I just about had a heart attack.

"What the hell?"

Kathleen laughed.

"Kathleen, what is this?"

"Pictures from Chloe, pal."

Yeah, I could see that. Except I couldn't believe my eyes. Chloe lying on a bed on her stomach. Her bottom smooth and tight and bare. Chloe and a friend, a girl, kissing. Chloe at the pool kissing a boy? girl? I couldn't tell for sure. Long hair obscured his or her face, but the hands cupping Chloe's rear end looked like they knew what they were doing.

"Kathleen, what is this?"

"Our daughter wanted to give us a little thrill. What do you think?"

My daughter wants to thrill us? I won't pretend I wasn't turned on, but I wondered where Chloe was going with this. Hell, where was Kathleen going?

"Here's another, John. Close your eyes."

I did. I heard some clicks and a rustle.

"OK, take a look."

I thought I was going to have a stroke. Or come in my pants. Or both.

It was a cabin of some sort, to judge by the rough logs and, god help me, moose heads on the walls. But that wasn't the central attraction.

No, the central attraction was Chloe, nude, lying on her side facing the fire, her back to the camera. She was mostly in shadow, but the light from the fire outlined the long smooth curves from her shoulder to her middle to her hip and thigh.

"Kathleen?"

"Yeah?"

"She's gorgeous."

"There's one more, John. Close your eyes again, OK?"

I heard another couple of clicks.

"OK, look."

Christ.

It was the same setting, but Chloe had rolled onto her back. Now the light from the fire outlined one breast, her erect nipple and her flat stomach. Her near leg was partly raised, her hip prominent, but not so high that I couldn't see a little of her pubic hair, just a bit. Her face was mostly in shadow, although I thought I saw a little smile.

"Kathleen, what did she say about these?"

Kathleen looked up at me. I leaned down and kissed her, first gently, then a little harder.

"She said she had something she wanted to show us. Well, show you, really, I think. She asked me if it was OK."

Kathleen kept her head tilted. I kissed her again.

"I told her I was sure you would like them. Was I right?"

I kissed her again. Her lips parted, and I was breathing hard before we separated.

"Yes."

Kathleen smiled.

"Good."

I'd spent the last week trying to figure out what I wanted with Chloe, with Kathleen. The first part was easy—I wanted to take Chloe to bed and do my best to pound her into the mattress and hear her scream at the moment of her climax. I wanted Kathleen there, too.

I was pretty sure Kathleen had her own thoughts about Chloe. Her smiles and Cheshire cat grins as we looked at the photos of Chloe told me as much. What's the harm, anyway? Chloe's an adult, at least nominally, and she seems pretty certain she knows what she wants. She's not even financially dependent on us anymore, thanks to two merit scholarships and a gift from her grandmother.

It would be one thing if she were in middle school, or something. Sure, I said to myself, that would be too young, wouldn't it? Also, if she'd never displayed any interest in me or Kathleen, that would be a different story, right? I opened a bottle of wine Friday night, late, the weekend before Thanksgiving. Had a glass. Pondered. Had another glass. Then another.

It didn't help. It only got me sloshed, and things weren't very pretty the next morning. At least it was Saturday.

When I'm stuck and meditation doesn't work, and for me it rarely does, I ask my spouse.

"Kathleen, be honest. What do you think Chloe wants? Is she really trying to seduce both of us, or me, or you, or none of the above?"

Kathleen gave me her, "Are you really that stupid" look. I get that a fair amount from her. This time, though, she somehow made it less sharp than usual.

"John, I think the answer's pretty clear, don't you? She wants you, yes, and I think she wants me, too, even though she hasn't quite made up her mind how fast she wants to go."

"How do you feel about that?"

Kind of an inane question, but I was serious.

"I feel horny."

Well.

"Me, too."

I poured myself another cup of coffee.

"She's not a virgin, right?"

"What do you think, John?"

"To judge by the photos it's not very likely, but who knows?"

"Exactly."

"I guess it doesn't matter, does it?"

"Exactly."

"I really want her, Kathleen."

Kathleen hugged me then let me go and smiled.

"You aren't the only one, pal."

"So, how do we handle this?"

Another tart look.

"Where's your brain? We let her lead, of course."

"She's coming home for Thanksgiving weekend, right?"

"Yup."

To: "Chloe" (chloe.wilson@xxx.edu)
Fm: jmwilson@xxxx.com
Subj: What's with the moose heads, anyway?

Hi sweetie—

Your mom and I love the photos, especially the ones of you in front of the fire. Want to tell us more about that night? You looked delicious, and I mean delicious!

Love,
Dad

To: "Dad" (jmwilson@xxxx.com)
Fm: chloe.wilson@xxx.edu
Subj: RE: What's with the moose heads, anyway?

Hi Dad—

I felt delicious, too! Ryan and Sylvia were there with me, and we got pretty mellow! It was so warm and comfy that we sort of decided to go bare and enjoy the fire.

Nothing happened, though! Well, almost nothing. Sylvia gave me a backrub. (Giggle!) Then Ryan gave Sylvia a backrub. All over! OMG! I'll tell you and Mom about it over Thanksgiving, OK?

Love,
Chloe

I printed off the exchange and gave it to Kathleen Sunday night. I liked the way she smiled when she finished reading Chloe's reply. I liked it even more when Kathleen grabbed me and took me to our bedroom and had her way with me.

Chloe's train arrived on time mid-afternoon on the Wednesday before Thanksgiving. A sea of people, bags, backpacks, overcoats and hats, but I saw her waving from the platform and it only took me a couple of minutes to push through the crowd and meet her at the gate.

She was smiling and happy and I responded to her extra squeeze with one of my own, not letting her overnight bag and backpack get in the way. Maybe I even lingered a little when I burrowed in past her scarf and kissed her on the side of her neck. I nuzzled her a little, too. Chloe snuggled in my arms.

I pulled back to look at her, my hands on her waist. Ever since she was little, I've looked into her grey eyes and I see her mother and I'm lost. This afternoon was no exception.

"Dad? Dad!"

I shook my head to clear it. I seemed to be doing that a lot.

"Are you there, Dad?"

Gave her one last squeeze and let her go.

"You bet, Chloe. Let's get out of here."

Twenty minutes later Kathleen and Chloe were hugging and squeezing just the way Chloe and I had done at the station. I saw a couple of neck nuzzles, too.

Chloe scooted upstairs to dump her stuff and shower, and I ordered the pizza. Extra cheese, extra sausage, side of hot wings, the works. It was cold and I was hungry. We'd have plenty of home cooking tomorrow.

Later that evening the pizza was gone and the three of us were sprawled in front of the fire, Chloe on her tummy, me on the sofa with Kathleen on the floor in front of me. I was about to speak, but Kathleen beat me to it.

"Sweetie, the moose cabin, you were going to tell us, right?"

Chloe turned from the fire, rolled on her side, her head on her arm. Her Zen smile was back.

"You guys sure you want to hear this?"

I laughed.

"You bet, Chloe."

"Mom?"

Kathleen didn't say anything. She snuggled back against me and I started to knead her shoulders. I couldn't see her face, but I bet she was smiling.

Chloe crawled right up to Kathleen. Her t-shirt was loose enough for me to watch her breasts swing as she moved. Inside my sweatpants I began to stiffen.

"Mom?"

I heard Kathleen giggle.

Chloe leaned forward and kissed Kathleen on her mouth. Then she worked around to Kathleen's neck. When Chloe turned her face up to me I saw "Yes" in her eyes and kissed her myself. Kathleen laughed and kissed Chloe once more, on the cheek this time.

"Sure, sweetie."

Chloe moved back in front of the fire and stretched out again on her tummy.

"It's Sylvia's uncle's cabin, and Sylvia's been going there since she was little. Her uncle lets anyone in the family use it whenever he's not there, which means she can go almost whenever she wants."

I was kneading Kathleen's shoulders again.

"So anyway, we'd just finished mid-terms and Sylvia asked me on Friday if I wanted to go with her and Ryan. We left Saturday morning and got there mid-afternoon.

"It was too cold to swim in the lake, but we hiked up the ridge behind the cabin and lay out in the sun for a while.

"We all took our shirts off."

Chloe gave us another of her Zen looks.

"Anyway, it's not like it was the first time Ryan saw us topless."

I felt Kathleen twitch. Chloe noticed.

"Hey, Mom, it's no big deal, you know? We even have 'Naked Thursdays' at school, where lots of kids run around nude. Not everyone takes a towel with him like you're supposed to, so you kind of have to watch where you sit in the dining hall, though."

I could have done without that image, thank you very much.

Chloe laughed.

"Anyway, we were all pretty relaxed by the end of the afternoon. Ryan grilled burgers for dinner. We each had a couple of beers while we ate and afterwards we ended up in front of the fire feeling all full and satisfied and warm and toasty."

Chloe shivered. Shook her head as if to clear it.

"Mmm. Yeah.

"Well, after a little bit Sylvia stood up and started taking off her clothes. That looked pretty good to me. To Ryan, too, I guess, because he was the first one naked. I could feel the fire on my bare skin. It felt good and made me a little tingly, too."

I pushed Kathleen a little forward so I could work down her spine a little. I heard little "Mmphs" and "Umms" and the like, so I figured she liked what I was doing. Chloe was watching her.

"Yeah, Mom. Feels good, right?"

Kathleen grunted. I kept working, only now I was going all the way down to the small of her back, then working back up her flanks to her shoulders, and down her spine once more.

"I was just lying there with my eyes almost shut, the fire warm, when Sylvia scooted over and started working on my shoulders, kind of like what Dad's doing right now with you,

Mom. I liked it and I guess it showed. Sylvia pushed me down on my tummy and straddled my butt and leaned on her hands as she worked on my back."

Kathleen sighed and leaned back against me and I made my touches gentle.

"I must have dozed off a little, because I was surprised when I felt Sylvia's hands on my bottom, and then down my legs, first one thigh, then the other. 'Everything OK, Chloe?' she asked me. I groaned, it felt so good. Then Sylvia was back sitting on my bottom and her hands were on my sides, going up and back."

Without thinking about it I'd started stroking Kathleen's flanks, then running my hands underneath her breasts. Chloe noticed.

"Yeah, Dad. That's what Sylvia was doing to me, only she wasn't touching me at first. Then before I knew it she slid her hands under me and cupped my boobs. And she kissed the back of my neck!

"Well, that was kind of getting me going, you know? We weren't like that, Sylvia and me, although we'd fooled around a little. I wasn't sure how far I wanted her to go, but I didn't have to worry. 'Check Ryan out, Chloe,' she said. I turned my head to look and, oh my, was Ryan ever interested. He was lying on his side, head propped up on one elbow, his other hand stroking himself. I'd never seen him that way before and it was turning me on like crazy.

" 'Join me, Chloe?' I shook my head. I was too chicken. Sylvia gave me another little kiss on my cheek and moved over to Ryan.

" 'OK, guy,' she told him. 'My turn.' She flopped down on her tummy and Ryan straddled her bottom and leaned forward to start with her shoulders, his cock right in the middle of her butt."

Kathleen sighed when I moved my hands up to cup her breasts. Chloe smiled.

"Nice, Mom?"

Kathleen sighed again.

"Maybe I should leave you guys alone, huh?"

Kathleen shook her head. I did, too, but I didn't take my hands off her breasts.

Chloe watched us. Or, rather, she watched my hands cup and press her mother's boobs. Then Kathleen spoke for the first time since Chloe had started her story.

"Yeah, sweetie. Keep going."

She turned her head to look up at me.

"You, too."

I ran my fingers across her nipples and went back to kneading her shoulders and her back.

"So, anyway, Ryan worked on Sylvia's shoulders and down her back a little, and he kept sliding his cock on her bottom while he did that."

This time when I got to the small of Kathleen's back I moved my hands around to her front and started back up, lifting the hem and taking her t-shirt with me. Kathleen held her arms up and I pulled it over her head and off and put it on the sofa beside me. Then I leaned forward again to cup her bare breasts and chafe her nipples with my thumbs and kiss the back and sides of her neck. I felt Kathleen shudder. She let out another little moan.

"Oh, god. Keep doing that."

I think that was Kathleen talking. Maybe it was Chloe, though, because she kept watching my hands on her mother's breasts. I'm not sure she realized she had one hand on her own breast right then. After a moment she dropped her hand and crawled over to us.

"I don't know if I can finish the story. You two aren't listening, are you?"

She leaned forward to kiss her mother lightly. I heard another sigh as they finished the kiss, then Kathleen held Chloe's head and returned the kiss. I held my hands steady, still cupping Kathleen's breasts.

Chloe drew back when the kiss was over. Took a deep breath, her face flushed. She smiled again.

"Wow, Mom."

"Yeah."

I took one hand off of Kathleen's breast and stretched to touch Chloe's cheek.

"Will you finish the story, Chloe?"

Kathleen looked up at me, her hand waving to take in what we were doing, us.

"Give Chloe a turn after the story, will you?"

I think I stiffened some more and my heart was racing, but I tried to keep my voice steady.

"Sure."

Kathleen smiled, put her hand up to touch my cheek.

"Good boy."

She turned back to Chloe.

"OK, sweetie, what happened next?"

A giggle.

"As if I couldn't guess."

Chloe laughed.

"You're right, Mom. Ryan worked on Sylvia for a bit more, then he gave it up, put his hands on either side of her, and started rubbing himself along her bottom. She was pushing back against him on each thrust. He was going faster when she shoved back hard. 'Stop!' He stopped. 'Let me turn over.'

"Ryan let her up and she flipped over on her back. Big smile as he straddled her again. He wasn't going to go inside her, I knew that, at least I didn't think he was, anyway.

"He didn't. 'OK, baby, come on me.' Ryan began thrusting again, his cock outside her pussy. After a minute he sat back on his heels and stroked himself a couple or three times and came all over her boobs and tummy. Got a little on her chin, too, I think. Then he fell forward on her and they were kissing."

Chloe stopped. Her Zen smile was back.

"That's all I remember, really. I was a little busy myself right then."

I was kneading Kathleen's boobs, my cock rigid in my sweats. Kathleen groaned. Pushed herself away from me.

"Hold on, tiger. It's Chloe's turn."

She waved at Chloe.

"OK, Chloe. He's all yours."

Chloe crawled over, another nice view down the front of her t-shirt. I could tell by her grin that she knew exactly where I was looking. She took Kathleen's place in front of me and snuggled back into my arms while Kathleen moved closer to the fire.

I wasn't sure how far Chloe or Kathleen wanted me to go or how to get there, so I started out easy. Too easy, it turned out.

"Dad!"

I kept going easy.

"Dad!"

"John, backrub, OK?"

"Got it."

I shifted into medium gear and started with Chloe's shoulders, just as I had with Kathleen, and moved down her spine and back up. Another round, but this time when I started back up I moved my hands to her sides and went back up to her shoulders. When I started down again, though, she did that little wriggle her mother was so expert at and before I realized it my hands were holding her breasts, her nipples sharp against my palms. I kneaded gently.

Instantly Chloe pushed back against me. It was pretty clear

she wanted my hands exactly where they were.

Let her lead.

When Chloe turned her face to me I kissed her, and I lingered this time. She liked that, apparently, because I felt her lips part and her tongue come out. I let mine touch hers, and we did the tongue dance for a bit. Both of us were breathing hard when we finished, and I resumed kneading her breasts. Her groan said she liked that, too.

To be honest, I wasn't sure where this was going, at least tonight, anyway, and I didn't want to push Chloe into something she didn't want, but at this point I wasn't in a mood to stop, either. In fact, after being hard so long I was getting less and less concerned by the second about who I would have in my arms when I came, and that moment was getting closer.

Let her lead.

Chloe saved herself and me from having to decide that particular question when she pulled out of my arms. She turned on her knees to face me and pulled my hands against her breasts. Then she pushed them down and I thought she wanted me to release her, but instead of letting go she put my hands under her t-shirt and tugged them up to her breasts again. Her boobs were warm and firm and I couldn't stop myself from rotating my palms against her stiff nipples.

I looked at her.

Let her lead.

For a moment her eyes were unfocused. Then she blinked and shook her head. Groaned. Looked down at my hands on her boobs. Smiled. Reached up to hold my head in her hands and kiss me.

"I'm sorry, Dad. Gotta go."

Let her lead.

I stifled my own groan and forced myself to smile.

"It's OK, sweetie. See you tomorrow. Sleep tight."

Chloe gave Kathleen a little wave and headed for the stairs.

Kathleen must have seen the desperation in my glance because in a second she was pulling my sweats and boxers down and closing her lips over me. I held her head as I pumped and spurted and sprayed down her throat.

My eyes were closed and I was savoring every movement of Kathleen's tongue as she gulped and swallowed when I heard a rustle. It was Chloe on the bottom step. As soon as she caught my eye she smiled, blew me a kiss and gave me a little wave as she turned and went on up the stairs. I raised my hand to wave back but she was already gone.

Kathleen looked up at me, licked a little bit off her lower lip.

"Kiss me."

I did.

"My turn."

She moved closer to the fire, flipped on her back, raised her hips and slid her shorts and panties down.

I did my best.

Thanksgiving afternoon I was smoothing our red tablecloth from Michoacán over the dining room table when Chloe walked in and grabbed me from behind and put her cheek against mine.

"Thanks, Dad."

I turned my head a little, and she kissed me.

"For what, Chloe?"

"Last night. For letting me go."

I moved out of her arms so I could turn and hug her. I held her tight.

"Oh, sweetie."

I kissed her.

"It's always up to you. You know that."

She smiled.

"Yeah, but thank you anyway."

"No worries. Help me with this?"

We had the tablecloth just right. Not much talk while we set out the silver and china and our Millennium crystal. I was fingering the tablecloth after we finished.

"So many good memories with this."

Chloe poked me.

"Yeah, Dad, I know. You say that every time you put it on the table."

"I mean it. They were fun meals and good times."

Chloe hugged me again. Her voice was soft this time.

"I know, Dad."

I gave her a swat.

"See if your mother needs help, OK?"

By the time we finished dinner that evening I was feeling the warmth of three glasses of wine, augmented by another kind of warmth as I enjoyed the play of candlelight on Kathleen and Chloe at the table, each showing a generous amount of cleavage, their skin fairly glowing, their curves nicely highlighted.

Chloe and I had cleanup duty. It's a small kitchen, so that's probably why we kept bumping into each other. Chloe giggling, me trying to keep from laughing, but another part of me ready to grab her and kiss her to within an inch of her life.

I brought a fresh bottle of wine with me when we joined Kathleen in the living room. We watched "Firelight" snuggled on the sofa, Chloe between us, her arm around Kathleen's shoulders. I was not-so-idly rubbing between Chloe's shoulder blades and dividing my attention between the screen and the smooth skin at the base of Chloe's neck.

After a couple of minutes of Sophie Marceau nude in a love scene in front of the fire, I couldn't resist any longer. I drew my fingernails across the base of Chloe's neck, then ran my hand up and under her ear. Then, fingers barely touching her, down the side of her neck. She shivered, and I leaned over and kissed her neck. She turned her head, her lips parted, her eyes saying "Yes" once more, and I kissed her. She backed off a little, her eyes not quite focused, her lips still parted but smiling.

"Mmm."

That sounded promising, and I leaned forward and kissed her again. Brought my free hand around and rested it on her bare skin above her breasts. She pressed herself against my hand, and I moved my hand down to cup one breast. That got another "Mmm," and she presented herself for another kiss. I obliged.

Kathleen's hand appeared from behind Chloe and covered Chloe's other breast. Chloe turned from me and kissed Kathleen, lingering. My pulse filled my ears and my stomach twisted, but not in pain. I was hard as a rock.

Kathleen pushed herself up from the sofa and cleared her throat.

"I'm going to slip into something more comfortable."

Chloe giggled.

"Me, too."

I figured I could either laugh at the cliché or keep my mouth shut and see what happened next. It wasn't a hard decision, and I knew it was the right one when Kathleen moved in front of me and turned her back.

"John, unzip?"

I did.

"Dad? Me, too?"

Staying in helpful mode, I unzipped Chloe. Couldn't stop myself from putting my hands on her bare warm shoulders. She and her mother stepped out of their dresses and folded them over the easy chair in the corner. The firelight turned their curves, nicely molded in brassière and panties, golden.

I disrobed to my boxers in two seconds. Socks off, too. I have no idea what the firelight did for me, but to judge by the looks I was getting from Kathleen and Chloe, the result wasn't too bad.

Kathleen stretched out in front of the fire.

"John?"

I straddled her butt and leaned forward just as I had done last night. Unclipped her bra. Slid my hands underneath as she rose up on her elbows, pulled her bra out from under her. Got an "Mmm" from her as I slid my hands back underneath her to cup her breasts.

"Do my back first, OK?"

I could do that, and in another moment or two she was grunting and "Mmphing" as I pressed my thumb into that spot just where her neck met her shoulder and held it there. Hurts a little but feels so good later. After that I moved on to her shoulder blades and worked down to the small of her back and back up again. I was mostly erect, sliding against her silky smooth panties while I massaged her.

Movement beside me, and I turned to see Chloe stretch her hand to Kathleen's cheek. Kathleen lifted her head to let Chloe kiss her. A long, slow kiss. Chloe broke away, lifted her head to me, and we had our own kiss, just as long, just as slow. I was rigid by now, pressing against Kathleen's bottom, my heart racing.

Took my hands off Kathleen and cupped Chloe's bare breasts. Don't know when she'd lost her bra, didn't care. I rubbed my thumbs across her nipples as I kissed her again.

"Hey!"

I looked down at Kathleen, who was trying to pout but looking like she was about to laugh.

"Sorry, babe. Back in a minute."

I dropped my head and suckled at Chloe's left breast. She pulled my head against her, and I moved to her right breast and flicked my tongue across the nipple. Put my mouth against her ear.

"Chloe, I'm going to make your mother come. Watch."

Chloe shivered.

I flipped Kathleen over on her back. Lay down full-length on her. Thrust myself against her pussy while I kissed her and did my best to get as much of my tongue inside her as I could. She retaliated immediately, and we dueled for a bit, my hand working on her breast, my cock pressed against her, even through two layers of cloth, mine and hers.

She was breathing hard when we finished. So was I. I worked my way down her neck giving her a light nip or two on the way to her breasts. Paid attention to her stiff nipples, and kept going down. Pulled her panties down and off. Between her legs Kathleen was fragrant and moist.

Her thighs pressed my head as I inhaled. I traced all of her with my tongue, finding her bump then leaving it and returning, leaving and returning. I was lost in her taste, her aroma, her moisture. Slipped two fingers into her heat, and felt her squeeze them. I crooked my fingers gently, and that got me another squeeze.

Kathleen had gone from pressing my head between her thighs to clamping me tight. I was trapped but I didn't care. I could die happy this way. Last night, today's meal, our cuddling in front of the fire, it was all foreplay and Kathleen was closer than I realized. Her pussy tightened around my fingers once more and again as her "Ah ah ah ah" became a long sigh and she exhaled.

I left my fingers to soak in her while I touched my tongue lightly on and around her clit. Let my fingers slip out and turned my head to lie flat on her mashed and wet fur. Inhaled. Exhaled.

I felt Chloe stretch out beside us. Her voice was soft, almost a whisper.

"Everything OK, Mom?"

A groan. Then I heard kissing. Someone giggled.

"Oh, yeah."

More kisses. I lifted my head to see Kathleen and Chloe locked together. Chloe was too tempting a target to pass up so I kissed her tummy and tongued her belly button. Ran my hand over her hip and down to her knee. She lifted her leg slightly and I moved up her thigh. Stopped short there and waited.

For a moment or two she didn't move. Then, as I moved my hand back to her hip, Chloe rolled onto her back and parted her legs.

"Kiss me, Dad!"

I hooked my fingers under her panties and stripped them off. Put my face between her thighs, licked her from bottom to top, knowing I'd hit her spot when I felt her twitch and heard her gasp.

Then I moved up her torso, kissing her nipples briefly before finding her mouth with mine and feeling my cock rigid against her center.

I drank her and tongued her, then pulled back. Her eyes were half open, her mouth soft and lips a little swollen. She was smiling. "Ripe," I thought to myself. My cock said, "Take her."

I smiled back and kissed her, hard. I raised my eyebrows. She nodded, barely moving her head. I still didn't know whether she was a virgin, and my cock didn't care either way and I knew it wasn't my business, but whether she was or not I didn't hear or see that green light yet. Sometime, maybe, but not now, not yet.

"Kiss me" meant exactly that. No more, no less.

"You bet, Chloe."

What works for Kathleen probably will work for her, I figured, and I had my face between her legs in a moment. She was hot, wet and waiting. All too soon, for me, anyway, she was bucking and thrashing, my head clamped between her thighs, her fingers in my hair, as she came again and again.

I showed her no mercy until she pushed me away, laughing. "Enough, Dad!"

I kissed her all over once more and tongued her clit in farewell. Shifted slightly and stripped my boxers off. Sat back on my knees, stroking my cock slowly. Kathleen was watching.

"Chloe, sweetie?"

Chloe, her eyes still soft and a little dreamy, looked up at Kathleen.

"Want to let your dad finish on you?"

Chloe smiled. Looked at me, eyes a little more focused now. "Dad?"

"What, sweetie?"

"Not inside me, OK?"

Let her lead.

"You got it, Chloe."

I kept stroking. I was going to come somewhere soon, that was for sure.

Kathleen leaned forward and kissed Chloe once more. Chloe reached up one hand to palm and cup Kathleen's breast.

"He'll come on your boobs, sweetie, if you want him to."

Chloe grinned.

"Yeah!"

She looked at me.

"OK, Dad?"

"You bet."

I straddled Chloe and began to stroke in earnest. Kathleen moved closer. In a moment she and Chloe were locked once more in a kiss, Kathleen's hand on Chloe's breast. They broke the kiss when they heard me grunt. Kathleen looked up at me.

"Now, John!"

I sprayed Chloe's face, chin and breasts. Deep shuddering breath as I collapsed to the side in Kathleen's arms. When I was able to focus again, Chloe was moving one hand slowly on her breasts, her other hand between her legs, a half-smile on her face. I leaned up on my elbow and kissed her.

"All OK, sweetie?"

A lazy smile.

"Oh, yeah."

Kathleen climbed half over me and kissed Chloe. She withdrew, still sort of on top of me, and giggled.

"Sure, Chloe?"

"Mom, you better believe it."

We cuddled in a heap for a bit until the fire began to die down and it was time for bed.

One more long hug from each of us, and Chloe headed upstairs. My eyes were on her taut smooth bottom until I glanced at Kathleen. She was watching Chloe just as carefully as I was.

Kathleen turned to me when Chloe disappeared.

"Come on, pal. You and I have unfinished business."

Kathleen was right, and once we were upstairs I took care of that when I kept my head between her smooth thighs again and my tongue stiff and moving just right and she jerked and moaned and thrust her pussy against my lips and tongue and came and came.

Then it was my turn again, and I pumped once more as Kathleen swallowed.

Sunday morning at the station Chloe pressed against me as I kissed her neck, her lips. She kissed me back, then nuzzled my ear. I responded, and she wriggled her hips.

"Was it what you wanted, Chloe?"

She smiled and gave me another wriggle.

"I can't wait for Christmas, Dad."

"Me, too, sweetie."

One last hug and a wave and she boarded the train and was gone.

2 Christmas

Hi. My name is Chloe, and I've read what Dad wrote about my Thanksgiving weekend at home with him and Mom.

"Tearing up her freshman dorm?" "Breaking hearts left and right?" Where does Mom get this stuff, anyway? I'm not a heartbreaker, and I don't dump people left or right or any way at all. That's not how I want to be treated, so I don't treat other people like that. "Cute daughter?" Well, yes, some people consider me cute (she said, modestly). They think Sylvia, my roommate, is cute, too. She and I look a lot alike, except she's blonde and I'm brunette.

Several of you asked Dad what happened at Christmas, and he told me I had to write it since it was my story. So, it's my turn now.

Where to start? Well, on the train back to school after Thanksgiving I let myself doze and I got all warm and toasty and even a little tingly as I remembered kisses from Mom and Dad and tongues and lips and how they wound me up tighter than ever before and then I tipped over into that rush and glow and it was so good I wanted to scream about it.

I didn't, but I bet I looked pretty silly. Mom and Dad didn't seem to mind. Dad had covered my face and neck and boobs when he came all over me, but he and Mom weren't even done yet! I don't think they know how much I can hear from their room when they get noisy. It was OK, though. I was busy myself right then, once more before I went to sleep.

The second half of Autumn Quarter, from midterms a couple of weeks before Thanksgiving until Christmas break, was a bitch. My papers, I had two of them, were due two weeks before finals, which meant I had a week to finish after I got back. I'd done all the research pretty much; all I had to do now was write.

"Start at the beginning, Chloe, go through to the end, and stop." I don't know how many times in high school Dad told me that when I complained about term papers, and I can hear him saying it now. I hate to admit it, but it was good advice.

Anyway, that first week back went pretty quickly. Except that most nights I fell asleep with my fingers busy as I remembered how warm the fire felt on my bare skin and Mom's soft lips caressing mine and how my palms loved holding her firm boobs. I hadn't touched Dad, not there, anyway, at least not yet, but I wondered how he would feel.

Friday afternoon I was finishing the final proof on my second and last paper and was about to e-mail it to the instructor when Sylvia came back from the library and banged open our door.

"Hey, Chloe! Want to go to the cabin with me and Ryan tomorrow?"

Ryan was right behind her. Big grin on his face.

Thinking what he was probably thinking about made me a little warm. Why not, I thought to myself. Next week was Dead Week, classes were over, pretty much, so it was going to be a grind. Why not have a little fun and blow off some steam first?

"Sure, unless you two want to be alone?"

Sylvia came over to my desk and took my face in her hands.

"Never. We both want you to come."

She giggled.

"With us, I mean."

Hah. That's what I was figuring. Did I want to?

Well, yeah, actually. I felt the start of a tingle. I looked over her shoulder at Ryan.

"What about you?"

He grinned.

"I really want you to come, Chloe."

"Ha ha, Ryan. Very subtle."

I looked at Sylvia again. The tingle I felt was a little stronger.

"You sure, sweetie?"

She kissed me.

"You bet, Chloe."

"OK. When are you leaving?"

"Right after lunch tomorrow, OK?"

"You bet."

This time it rained all the way up to the cabin. No sunning on the rocks, topless or not. I shivered when Sylvia opened the cabin door and I stepped inside. No way I was taking off my clothes this time.

"Chloe, help me bring in some wood, will you?"

I followed Ryan around to the woodshed. It was freezing and by my third trip I was soaking wet, even with my rain parka. The good news was that we now had enough wood inside to go through the night, if we wanted to.

An hour later, things were looking up. Ryan's fire crackled, my dry clothes were soft against my skin, I'd piled our stuff in the corner, and the stew Sylvia was heating smelled delicious, even if it had come out of a can, and it was making my stomach growl and my mouth water. I almost said "drool," but it wasn't quite that bad. Yet.

The shivers had turned to flutters in my stomach, and they weren't food-related. Look, I'll just come out and say it. I'm a virgin. I mean, I've never had a cock in my pussy. I've had some other experiences, though. I may not have gone all the way yet, but I've sure had fun getting part of the way "there."

One thing I can't deny. I'm kind of focused on that "all the way" thing. Not obsessed about it, no way. No. Some girls snicker when they talk about it. What's the difference, they say, between a guy's dick in your mouth and one in your pussy, anyway? There is to me. At least I think so. Well, yeah, maybe I am obsessed about this after all. A little, at any rate.

I told Mom and Dad that Sylvia and I weren't like that, which is true, but it's not like we haven't fooled around a little. I mean, where do you think those pictures of my bottom and kissing in the pool that I sent to Mom and Dad came from, anyway? Plus, Ryan's cock isn't the first one I've seen, hard or soft, and Dad wasn't the first guy to come all over me. There was Paul last year, and David earlier, and they were fun. I'm not complaining, but there's no need to spend any more time on them right now.

Dad wasn't the first person to eat me crazy, either.

So, I may not be Little Miss Experienced, but I've had a good time learning what I like. All in good time, I say, and this weekend was shaping up to be a good time. For what, I wasn't sure yet.

My tingle was back, along with a seriously warm feeling in the right spot. What I'm trying to say is that I was getting really hungry, and not just for Sylvia's stew.

Another hour or so later the cabin was warm and we were fed and happy once again. We were working on our second bottle of red when I stood up.

"I have an announcement."

It was the wine speaking, I think.

"I'm going to get naked."

The look on their faces was priceless. Then Sylvia grinned and Ryan adjusted himself. That was promising, I thought.

Sylvia's grin turned into a smirk.

"You go, girl!"

So I got naked. Stretched, hands behind my head. Twisted from one side to the other. Not trying to show off, really. OK, maybe a little. Mostly I was trying to make like a cat. I felt the muscles in my neck and back pull and the tension started to melt. That felt seriously good.

"I'll join you."

In a moment, Sylvia was just as bare as I was and she stood and stretched with me, our backs extended, our boobs out, our arms as high as we could get.

Ryan? His tongue was halfway to the floor and in his loose sweats he was signaling his approval in the traditional male manner. Good.

Sylvia and I paused to look at each other. Great minds think alike, and it must have been Ryan's best wet dream to be attacked by two gorgeous, if I may say so, nude women who were kissing every inch of his bare skin as they uncovered it.

We ended up in a laughing heap on the rug in front of the fire, Ryan's sweats and boxers around his ankles, Sylvia's hand on his erect cock and mine on his chest as I did my best to get my tongue down his throat. Smart boy that he was he'd decided resistance was futile, and his hand on my right boob was doing very welcome things for my tingles.

After we sorted ourselves out things got even better, although I'm actually kind of hazy on exactly what happened that evening. The details, I mean. I guess the wine hit me kind of hard. I knew I was safe. Ryan and Sylvia wouldn't hurt me. That's what made me want to do stuff—knowing they wouldn't go any farther than I wanted to go.

Relishing the wet tongue between my legs and flicking against my clit, circling my lips, stabbing me oh so sweetly; returning the favor, first with Sylvia until she arched and tensed, then with Ryan, his cock warm and stiff with skin smooth and soft, full and round in my mouth.

Getting hotter and hotter watching Ryan growl and thrust lion-style behind Sylvia. Her grunts and moans and my fingers working my clit winding my spring like nobody's business until I was so tight I burst. My scream came from nowhere and forced itself out and I let it go where it wanted.

Sylvia back between my legs later on, my clit loving her tongue, my pussy clamped on her two fingers until I was lost and gone and so warm and so relaxed I never wanted to move ever again.

Waiting beside Sylvia on our backs, fingers linked, watching Ryan powering between her legs again, feeling each thrust as Sylvia jerked and tensed. Then Ryan's hot splashes on my tummy as he emptied himself over me.

Giggling. Maybe it was me? Ryan? No, guys don't giggle. Sylvia. It must be Sylvia. Catching. Laughter. Weak as kittens then, both of us.

Ryan again, fat and smooth and warm in my mouth. Pulsing once more, not so much this time, as I swallowed. Cleaning, licking, letting him slip out when he got small again. Sylvia holding me tight from behind while he finished, her hands warm and making small circles on my boobs.

Sleepy. On my side facing the fire, Sylvia spooned against me. Her hand warm on my hip. Wanted it on my boob but too sleepy to ask. Ryan behind her, I think.

Memory of movement in the night. Small noises. Whimpers, a moan. Without conscious thought my hand went between my legs once more, tracing up and down, circling my spot. Wanting harder, then softer, faster, slower, bursting through just as the movement beside me became frantic. Afterwards splayed, wanton, open to the air. Almost hoping someone would fill me. Almost.

Then it was cold again. Fire almost gone. Bundled up, the three of us, using every blanket in the room.

In the bright morning, sleepy at first but fast waking up with Sylvia's lips on mine, wet, warm, her tongue greeting me. Throbbing, our hands busy on each other, Ryan watching. Afterwards I was awake, watching the sunlight splash on the sofa. Boneless after my peak. Sylvia's mouth leaving mine as she turned over on her back and opened to Ryan and he straddled her and eased himself into her wet hot mouth.

I got the news on the first day of finals. Holy cow! We were spending Christmas at Lake Tahoe this year!

If she'd taken a partnership when it was offered back then, by now Mom's bonus plus share in the profits would have been well into six figures, Dad told me. As it was her bonus was less than that, although he wouldn't tell me exactly how much, but it was fat enough they decided to splurge a little.

Lake Tahoe, yeah!

Oh, and there was more. Dad told me I could invite Ryan and Sylvia for part of the time, if I wanted to and they wanted to. After my last weekend at the cabin with them, I did. I wondered what Dad and Mom were up to, but when I asked Dad he laughed and told me to ask Mom. So I did.

"Congratulations, Mom! On your bonus, I mean."

"Thank you, sweetie."

"Um, Mom?"

"Yeah?"

"Are you sure about having Ryan and Sylvia there?"

"You bet, Chloe."

"I mean, Mom, I've gotten pretty close with them, you know?" She laughed.

"That's OK, sweetie. Really. You're all adults. Your dad and I aren't going to say anything."

Another pause. Something that sounded like a giggle.

"I mean, not anything, Chloe. Your dad isn't the jealous type, you know?"

"Mom? Is there something you're not telling me?"

This time she laughed.

"Chloe, there's plenty we don't tell you. Parents have their privacy, too."

She stopped for the longest minute.

"Mom, still there?"

"Oh, yes, sweetie. What I mean is, our little adventures last summer and at Thanksgiving aren't the first time your dad and I have experimented a little."

She laughed again.

"I'm not going to tell you what we did in college, either."

I know kids are supposed to be grossed out hearing things like that about their parents, but I wasn't. Quite the contrary, in fact.

"Mom? A hint, OK?"

"Sweetie, I mean it. We have our privacy just as you have yours. Our friends do, too."

Another pause.

"OK, I'll tell you this much. Remember when you stayed with your grandmother a couple of years ago while we went to the Caribbean with Mr. and Mrs. Robinson? Remember? We showed you some photos."

Oh, yeah. You bet I did. Especially the ones of them skinny-dipping.

"Well, we did more than skinny-dip together."

"Oh."

My turn to pause. I giggled.

"Pretty sure Ryan and Sylvia might like this."

"Remember, sweetie, no expectations from anyone, right?"

"Right."

"Good luck on exams, Chloe."

"Thanks, Mom."

Thank god for Finals Week care packages. Sylvia and I made out like bandits. Ryan not so much, but we shared. We were munching away one evening when I told them about Lake Tahoe. They jumped at my invitation. Sylvia's family were going to spend the holidays with distant relatives in Sweden (Huh? Brrr!), and Ryan's folks were going to Florida, so Ryan and Sylvia were going to come up for a couple of nights just before Christmas, then fly to Florida on the 26th to be with Ryan's family.

I told them about my conversation with Mom and her talk of "experimenting."

"Guys, I want to be clear about this. Things might get a little weird, you know? Maybe nothing happens, maybe something does. No expectations, right?"

Sylvia looked at Ryan. Ryan looked at me. Sylvia answered for both of them.

"Chloe, you already know we like to play. Ryan does, especially. He's seen that photo of your mom that you keep on your desk, too."

Ryan grinned.

"Yeah. The cabin, too."

Sylvia poked him. Leaned over and kissed me.

"How do you feel about it, Chloe, really?"

I felt a tingle. I knew how I felt about it. No expectations. No requirements. Just possibilities. I hoped she could hear the smile in my voice.

"I like it."

"Done."

It was snowing the afternoon of December 23rd when we picked up Ryan and Sylvia at the airport and drove to the cabin. Well, it was really more a chalet than a cabin. I mean, when the "cabin" has a huge kitchen, a sauna and a gigantic hot tub, a full set of skis for eight and several pairs of snowshoes, in my book it's a chalet, not that I've had that much first-hand experience with chalets. By the time we'd finished unloading their stuff, there was no visibility outside. The radio said the airport was closed and everyone was advised to stay off the roads to let the plows do their work. That was OK. We'd stocked up with enough food to last a week, and the power was still on. No worries for us.

We all ended up in the hot tub that night. The tub was indoors, just inside the sliding door to the deck. Nobody—in California, anyway—wears a swimsuit in a hot tub, and trying to watch everyone at once to see who was checking whom out kept me really busy. Dad clearly appreciated Sylvia's curves, and Ryan was doing his best to not ogle Mom and failing miserably. I could tell she knew and I saw the beginnings of a smile once or twice, but she kept quiet. In fact, she got her own eyeful of Ryan and I'm pretty sure she liked what she saw.

We got out after a while, dried off and hit the sack, or our separate sacks, even if Ryan, Sylvia and I decided we'd sleep in front of the fire.

Nothing happened that night. We were all too tired.

The next morning, December 24th, Mom and I were having an early cup of coffee in the breakfast nook, the sunlight reflecting off the snow outside after yesterday's storm almost too bright for comfort.

"Mom, I don't know what I want."

I was thinking about tonight, Christmas Eve.

"I've done some stuff, I have. I mean, I know I want to do some other things, um, but I'm not sure."

I was kind of sounding like a little kid here but I didn't know how else to say it. Mom was grinning, except I knew she wasn't being mean. She was Mom, and she loved me. She reached to take my hand in hers.

"I know."

She squeezed my hand.

"Chloe, of course it matters. What you want matters."

She looked out the window for a minute.

"Are you a 'virgin' even if you've 'done stuff'? Do you care? Is that how you see things? See yourself? Are you looking for a label?"

I thought about that for a minute. One thing I love Mom and Dad for is that they never ever let up on me. Oh, sure, they set limits, but they always insisted that I try as hard as I could, even as they stood back and let me work my way through whatever it was. I hated that. Until I loved them for it.

The more I turned the "virgin" thing over in my mind the more I realized I cared a lot about it, yes, but I was starting to see that I got to decide what was important and how and where and when and who. No labels. Not any more. Just me, Chloe, and what felt right.

I decided I would know when it was the right time, and from now on I wouldn't worry so much about it.

An hour later Mom and Dad and I were outside, ready to go.

"Last one there's a rotten egg!"

With that Dad set off on skis through the forest. He was heading slightly uphill toward an angle of the ridge behind our chalet. He was moving quickly now through the powder that fell overnight, but I was pretty sure it was going to be a slog before we got there. No matter—I was rested and wound up and ready for anything.

Mom was right behind him, me behind her. Ryan and Sylvia hadn't moved from their deck chairs in the bright sun, coffee cups in hand, even when I'd challenged them to join us.

"You guys going to veg out the whole time?"

"Nah. Just this morning. We need to catch up on our sleep."

Ryan elbowed Sylvia and wiggled his eyebrows. She shot him a "Down, boy" look, but I could tell she was thinking about some more "sleep" herself.

Let them be, I thought to myself. More Mom and Dad time for me, and I set off.

Dad got there first, of course. Mom second, and I brought up the rear as usual. My heart was pumping to beat the band, the air cold and clear and delicious enough to bite. Is this what exhilaration feels like? If so, I wanted more. It was different from arousal, so self-centered and self-contained. No, this was outward-reaching and I felt myself expanding into the trees, the rocks, the sky.

I came back to earth when Mom hugged me tight. Our lips were cold at first touch, then warmer and wetter. At the touch of her tongue I withdrew and burrowed under her parka and sweater to kiss her neck. She whimpered until I returned to her lips and invaded. Some serious heat here. Even more when I felt someone press against me from behind and Dad's hands cupped my breasts. My nipples liked that, even through the layers of wool and nylon separating them from his palms.

I went on kissing Mom for a moment or two, the filling in their sandwich. It was Mom's turn to cup my breasts when I turned to kiss Dad. That felt just as good, and I wriggled against Dad to show him how much I liked being in his arms, too.

The three of us were grinning when we finally broke apart. First Mom then Dad kissed my cheek.

"Chloe!"

"Mom. Dad."

Dad took an exaggerated deep breath, his back arched.

"Nothing like exercise outdoors, right?" Mom and I hit him, one from each side.

I stopped dead when I reached the deck after stacking my skis against the house. Dad ran into me from behind, his hands on my hips. In a couple of moments he pressed himself against my bottom once more as he realized what he was seeing through the window.

Sylvia and Ryan didn't see us. That's because Ryan, sitting on the side of the hot tub, had his eyes closed. Sylvia didn't notice because she was concentrating on Ryan's cock filling her mouth as she gobbled and sucked and stroked him.

I felt Dad's hands under my sweater as he moved up to palm my boobs, his hands still warm since he'd just removed his gloves. He started to thrust against my butt as his fingers found my nipples. I closed my eyes until I heard Mom's "Yes!" and opened them to see Sylvia pull her mouth from Ryan's cock. Her hand jacked him as he throbbed and spurted on her face.

She milked him until his spurts subsided. Then Ryan saw us and smiled and waved. Sylvia turned her head and gave me a little wave, too. By the time Mom, Dad and I had hung up our coats inside, the two of them were seated side-by-side in the tub, Sylvia's face all clean, smiles on their faces.

We spent the afternoon at the outdoor ice rink, laughing, falling down, helping each other back up, racing as fast as we could. For some of us that wasn't very fast. Ryan and Dad were aces, Sylvia, too, and Mom and I kind of spazzed along at our own speed around the rink. Sometimes my hand would find someone's rear end, once or twice someone's front, a breast or two, even, but no one seemed to mind. Other hands found me and felt me up, and I wriggled and tried to show whoever it was how much I liked that.

It was late afternoon and getting dark and starting to snow again when we got back to the chalet and piled into the hot tub. I was kind of lazing away, leaning against Sylvia, my eyes half-closed, liking the way the water was touching me everywhere, when Sylvia spoke, her lips practically against my ear.

"Look at your mom. I think she's going to get lucky later, if she wants to."

I pulled away and looked across at the others. Mom had squeezed herself between Dad and Ryan. They certainly weren't complaining and nothing much seemed to be happening, except Ryan's fingers were rubbing the back of Mom's neck slowly. I saw that Dad's hand was underwater, also moving slowly. Mom had a little smile on her face, her eyes closed.

"You OK with that, sweetie? I mean, with Ryan and all?"

Sylvia kissed my cheek first, then brushed my lips with hers.

"Why not? You and I can watch and amuse ourselves, too."

That sounded pretty good to me, and I returned her kiss, my hand coming around to slide up to her breast and tease her nipple.

All too soon, Dad herded us out of the hot tub and into the snow, flakes still falling. Screams, yowls, yells as the snow hit warm skin. He made us roll side-to-side at least twice. Then he started throwing snowballs. Ryan jumped to our defense and we all piled on, a bunch of naked people throwing snow around, and pretty soon Dad surrendered.

"OK everyone, sauna."

We trooped into the sauna, skin reddened, breathing hard, and spread out on towels. My pores opened up and it was glorious.

Dad threw some cold water on the coals once or twice, but we skipped the birch thing, the part where you swat each other with birch twigs.

Back out to the snow for another roll. Whatever doesn't give you a heart attack makes you stronger, I was thinking. A fast roll, and I pushed my way to the front to be first back in the sauna. Top shelf for me this time, my skin flushed.

We finished off with another dip in the hot tub, a quick one, and showers all around. Then it was on to a light dinner, salty stuff, plenty of water to replenish what we'd lost. We'd have a monster meal tomorrow, if I was any judge of what Mom had in mind.

We were all enjoying the fire after dinner, me trembling, a funny feeling, not a bad one, in my stomach, my heart going a little faster all because I was pretty sure what was coming and I wondered if Mom and Dad and Ryan and Sylvia felt the same way. I couldn't tell for sure, although the way Dad had his arm around Mom and his hand on her left boob suggested I wasn't alone.

I stuck to mineral water after dinner. I was determined to stay more alert than I had been at the cabin that night with Sylvia and Ryan. The others had wine, but remembering the evening later I realized it hadn't slowed them down much at all.

Dad emptied his wine glass and stood up.

"Who's up for a massage?"

Mom, Sylvia and I spoke at once.

"Me!"

It was easy to strip off what little clothing we'd put on for our post-sauna meal.

"Ryan, you help me with Kathleen, OK?"

Sylvia blew Ryan a little kiss when he looked at her. Yup, Mom was going to get lucky tonight, no doubt about it. I shivered.

Who knew that kissing was a massage technique? Apparently Ryan and Dad did, because I don't think Dad had been up and down Mom's back twice before he scooted down, leaned over, and kissed her between her shoulder blades.

Ryan was helping by lying on his stomach in front of Mom and kissing her. They broke for a moment and grinned at each other. Then their mouths were locked together again and I suspect tongues were involved. This seemed to be exactly the kind of massage Mom was expecting and hoping for.

Meanwhile, Sylvia was leaning back on her elbows beside me, her legs slightly parted.

"Chloe?"

She didn't have to ask twice. I wasn't going to be left out and I wasn't going to leave Sylvia all alone, either. Her lips were soft and a little wet, and when I worked my way down to her center, she was wet there, too. Juicy tonight. I like peaches and I went at her kind of like I go after a peach, only I used my lips and tongue and not my teeth.

I paused for a moment when out of the corner of my eye I saw Dad lift and pull Mom's hips up. She got on all fours and let Dad slip into her from behind while she opened her mouth to Ryan's cock and let Dad's thrusts do the work with Ryan.

A growl from Sylvia told me I needed to pay attention again. I was licking and sucking, a finger inside her as she worked higher and higher and I lost myself in her aroma and her wetness until I felt her peak as she quivered and her pussy tensed and released once, twice and I powered her through a third contraction. I was going for a fourth when she pushed my head away, laughing. I looked up, her juices warm and sticky on my face.

"Give up?"

"Enough!"

"Chicken."

She laughed.

"You'll beg me for mercy before I'm finished with you, Chloe."

I jerked my head in the direction of Mom and Dad and Ryan, and we watched as Ryan pulled back from Mom and erupted on her face. Dad had already finished, it looked like, although he was still as far inside her as he could get.

Washcloths all around, and another bottle of wine, heat from the fire making it easy to stay bare as we rested. I decided I'd earned a glass of wine.

My wine-inspired glow got hotter when Mom turned and kissed me. It was the polite thing to do to kiss her back, of course, and that made me burn. I broke from her mouth and moved to her neck and kept moving. I found a nipple in short order, a stiff one, and Mom's hand on the back of my neck held me tight against her and I had nowhere to go.

After a moment, though, I let Mom stretch out on the floor and surrendered to what was shaping up to be my pussy-eating role this evening. I wasn't complaining, far from it. Mom was primed from her earlier round, no surprise there, and she rewarded my efforts with little grunts, her thighs clasping and releasing my head as I licked and sucked and tasted her juices and Dad's cum. All of a sudden Mom shuddered in her own climax, and when I looked up her belly she had one hand on her right breast, twisting her nipple.

I didn't see it until Mom released me, but if I was doing a lot of the eating this was Sylvia's night to be eaten. I wondered whether she liked what Dad was doing more than me, and quickly decided it didn't matter. I'd lick her and suck her and eat her again and again until I got it right, no question.

Meanwhile, once Mom recovered she pushed me back and she settled between my legs, her tongue beginning its magic and my pussy, yearning to be touched and stroked and licked, got what it wanted. My eyes closed and my world became wet and hot and, well, slurpy, as Mom's tongue found corners I didn't know were there. Once when I opened my eyes I saw Ryan knee-walk up behind Mom, his hand on his freshened cock. Mom paused when he entered her, but she resumed in a moment and the rhythm of Ryan's thrusts provided a counterpoint to Mom's tongue.

I gave up trying to see or hear or figure out what was going on around me as Mom gave me two fingers and crooked them gently and pressed up and her tongue flicked me up and up and over the edge and down the other side and I kind of disappeared for a while.

When I came back I didn't know where I was, but it was the most beautiful place I could imagine. Every muscle at rest, warm and, yes, a little sweaty, but that part didn't matter. My middle, my pussy, my cunt, was satisfied, even if by tongue and lips and fingers only, no cock yet, Mom's head cradled between my thighs, her fingers still soaking in me, her head turned to the side, resting on my wet and matted pubic hair, just a hint of a smile on her face.

When I lifted my head I saw Dad with his head between Sylvia's splayed thighs, mirroring Mom between mine. His efforts had been wildly successful, to judge by Sylvia's loopy grin. I myself had been thoroughly eaten, even better than at Thanksgiving and at the cabin, and right then I didn't have a care in the world.

Ryan's eyes met mine when I looked beyond Mom. He'd collapsed over Mom's trim bottom when he finished, but I don't think Mom minded. He grinned, gave me a little wave with one hand.

Dad stood up.

"Bedtime. Kathleen? Chloe?"

I wanted more with Mom and Dad, even if I didn't yet know exactly what I wanted more of, so it wasn't hard to choose.

"Merry Christmas, everyone!"

I turned and followed Mom and Dad to their room, a quick shower, and bed.

In the night, I don't know when, I woke to Dad straddling Mom, her hands cradling his balls, her mouth working him, swallowing him almost to the root. God, how does she do that, anyway?

She let Dad slip from her mouth and turned to me. "Want to help me, Chloe?"

Echoes of Sylvia's invitation earlier at the cabin, but things were different now.

My heart pounding, partly in fear, but I was also getting wetter by the second and my nipples were hard, so partly in hunger as well. Oh yes, did I ever want to help, at least this much, anyway, and I realized some things that seemed certain earlier were starting to feel negotiable.

"Yeah!"

I opened my mouth as Dad settled in above me, and I stuck my tongue out to let him slip in easily. He was warm and firm and he filled my mouth. I couldn't see his face very clearly, no, but I could see his grin. I let him out for a second.

"Dad, everything OK?"

He laughed.

"Even better than that, sweetie. Tell me if I push too hard, OK?"

He didn't need to worry. I wanted him there, I wanted him to fuck my mouth and use me. I wanted to feel him round and fat and hot and I wanted him to fill me. In a second he was back inside and I had one hand jacking him, the other cradling his balls, my tongue keeping him nice and slippery.

I held my head still and he moved faster and faster and he was really fucking me now, fucking me, fucking my mouth, his hand in my hair, me squeezing his balls gently, until he grunted and pulled out and he shot hot and wet and sticky on my cheeks, my mouth, my neck, even on my boobs, and my skin burned where his stuff, his cum, touched me and covered me.

Then he was shrinking and all of a sudden I could hold him entirely in my mouth. I suckled gently, letting him rest on my tongue, cleaning him. He eased to my side, and his strong hands turned my face to him and he was kissing me, his tongue wandering a little and I was lost in the kiss until something hot and wet touched my breasts, neck and face and Mom cleaned me with a washcloth.

48

I fell asleep cuddling with Mom, Dad pressed against my backside.

Christmas morning came too early and I could already tell it was going to be another bright icy day. Maybe it was too early, but waking up between Mom and Dad made up for some of that. Lying between them, I knew I was loved and safe.

I knew something else, too.

"Mom, are you awake?"

I heard her sleepy, "Yes," as her eyes opened. I kissed her, a light touch of my lips on hers, and rolled to face Dad.

"I'm ready, Dad."

I pressed myself against him and kissed the side of his neck once, twice, three times. I closed my eyes and nestled in his arms and pushed my center against his growing erection. Mom cuddled me from behind, her breasts against my back, one leg over my hip, her fur a little scratchy against my bottom.

I heard her sweet whisper as her warm palm cupped my breast.

"Merry Christmas, Chloe."

I didn't know you could laugh and cry and kiss someone or someones all at the same time, but you can and I did.

When we quieted a little I kissed Dad again, this time slowly and carefully and thoroughly, very thoroughly, to make sure he got the message. When I released him and opened my eyes his were inches from mine and I saw love and warmth there. Desire and hunger, too.

I smiled and rolled onto my back and opened my thighs.

Dad mounted me.

3 Easter

CHLOE AND I FLIPPED A COIN to see who would tell you all about Easter. I won, so it's my turn again but don't worry, Chloe will have plenty to say.

"Chloe! What ...?"

She cut me off that Saturday morning by launching herself into my arms laughing and giggling and squeezing. She hung onto me until she heard Kathleen's voice from the kitchen.

"John, who ... Chloe?"

Chloe released me and stepped into Kathleen's arms and plastered herself against Kathleen and burrowed and nuzzled into Kathleen's neck.

I moved behind Chloe and put my arms around her and Kathleen. Chloe wriggled her bottom against me for a moment before she spun around to hug me again and nuzzle me, too. She pulled her head back and kissed me on the lips.

"Hi, Dad! Hi, Mom!"

She laughed at our faces.

"Surprise, huh?

"I was thinking about Christmas and wanted to see you guys again."

We must have looked a little puzzled, maybe even more apprehensive than puzzled. I knew what I was thinking—Lake

49

Tahoe. Christmas. Other than a quick, "I'm back on campus, everything's OK," we hadn't heard anything from her since she'd returned to school three weeks ago.

"Mom, Dad, it's fine. Really. I loved all of it."

Bright sun on Christmas morning. Icy outside, warm and humid and smooth and soft and wet in our bed. Thrusting into Chloe again and again, Kathleen beside me kissing Chloe and tweaking Chloe's nipples as Chloe writhed and spasmed and whimpered beneath me until she convulsed right before I finished inside her.

Late that afternoon, Chloe grunted and moaned when I took her a second time in front of the fire while beside us Ryan filled Kathleen's mouth and Sylvia watched and played with herself. Afterwards, Chloe on her tummy on the rug, her bare bottom inviting our continued attention. I shook my head to clear my memories.

"We did too, sweetie."

Kathleen stroked Chloe's hair as she spoke.

"Coffee, Chloe?"

"Yeah!"

In front of the gas fire our girl stretched out her legs, her back against the big easy chair, coffee on the carpet beside her. She smiled.

"I know we haven't talked very much about Lake Tahoe."

Another smile. Looked at her mother, then at me.

"I wanted you to know I loved it. All of it. I love you. I love you both."

"Oh, Chloe!"

Kathleen was out of her chair in a flash and hugged Chloe.

"Sylvia and Ryan did, too, Mom."

Chloe gave a little giggle then, and I swear I saw Kathleen blush. Thinking about Ryan coming all over her face, I was sure, and I guess it showed somehow. Chloe noticed.

"Yeah, Dad. Like that."

"So, Chloe, what's the deal? How're you? How are Ryan and Sylvia doing?"

"Dad, you too, Mom. Everything's OK with me. I'm fine. Ryan and Sylvia are fine. Everybody's good. Really."

She paused. Looked down for a moment. I'm not sure if it's possible, but I'd swear she was caught between a frown and a grin and I think the grin was winning.

"I'm not sure what happens next, you know?"

My turn to look away, out at our garden, the sky leaden on this January morning. Kathleen spoke for both of us.

"What do you mean, Chloe?"

"Mom, I don't know exactly. Really, I don't. I'm starting to see this guy, Robert, and I like him a lot, you know?"

Kathleen brushed a lock of Chloe's hair back behind her ear. Touched her lips to Chloe's cheek.

"Sweetie, and?"

Chloe fiddled with her coffee. Took a sip. Put the mug back on the carpet. Looked out the window. Her grin appeared again, but only for a second.

"Mom, I liked what we did, really."

She went back to fiddling with her coffee. Maybe it had the answer, but I didn't think so.

Kathleen stroked Chloe's hair again and kissed her cheek once more.

"Chloe, are you worrying about what your dad and I are thinking? That we'll be angry or disappointed or something?"

Chloe looked up.

"No, Mom!"

Kathleen glanced at me. Turned to Chloe and hugged her awkwardly from the side, pulling Chloe halfway into her lap. Kathleen continued to stroke Chloe's hair, gentling her.

"Sweetie, no. You don't ever have to worry about us. Not ever."

She kissed Chloe's cheek again.

"Never."

Petting Chloe.

"Chloe, your dad and I loved what happened at Thanksgiving and then at Christmas at Lake Tahoe. Loved it. Loved you, loved Ryan, and we loved having Sylvia, too."

Kathleen glanced at me. I smiled and nodded.

"Your mom's right, Chloe. Loved it."

"Sweetie, we love you. You're all grown up and almost on your own. You'll make your own choices."

Another kiss.

"Whatever you choose now or in the future is fine by us. We love you."

One more kiss.

"What I'm trying to say, Chloe, is that we'll follow your lead, whatever that is."

Kathleen giggled. Kissed Chloe again, this time on her lips but not too hard.

"Whatever that is, sweetie."

I cleared my throat.

"That's it, Chloe. What your mom said. Don't worry about us."

Chloe had her eyes closed, but her face was clearer and I was pretty sure she was listening to everything Kathleen said. When she spoke, it was almost a whisper.

"It's not what you think. Not at all."

Chloe opened her eyes and looked at each of us. Her grin was back, albeit maybe a little uncertain of its welcome.

"He likes to watch."

Kathleen and I looked at each other. Once more Kathleen spoke first.

"Who does, Chloe? Watch what?"

I saw a smile replace the grin. The smile got broader.

"Robert. Rob."

"Watch what?"

"Me. Sylvia. Ryan."

The light dawned.

"He takes pictures, too."

I had to adjust myself. As I did so, Chloe pulled Kathleen down and kissed her on the lips. Pushed herself up and shook her head as if to clear her thoughts.

"Thanks, Mom. Thanks, Dad. Back in a sec."

With that Chloe got to her feet and left the room. We heard water running in the bathroom. Kathleen turned to me.

"John?"

I shrugged.

"I don't know. We'll find out soon enough, I guess."

I rose and went over to Kathleen. Knelt and kissed her once, twice. A third time, thoroughly.

"You nailed it, Kathleen."

I hugged her for a second before I went back to the sofa.

"OK guys, let's try again."

A freshly-washed Chloe stood in the hall entryway. This time she came over and sat beside me on the couch and took my hands in hers.

"Thank you."

She brushed her lips against mine.

"I'd like to bring Rob to meet you. Maybe over the long weekend in February?"

I glanced at Kathleen. We spoke together.

"Sure, Chloe."

"Maybe tonight you'd like to see some of his pictures?"

"You bet, sweetie."

I hugged Chloe as I spoke.

"OK. Gotta go. I told Diana I'd meet her at the mall for lunch. See you tonight!"

With that she was out of the house and gone, leaving me, at least, with a mixture of uncertainty and excitement. Uncertainty about this Rob, or Robert, guy, excitement at what Chloe might show us tonight. When I looked over at Kathleen, I thought I saw the same feelings. Kathleen spoke first.

"So, John, where are we?"

"Honestly? I don't know. Really, I don't."

"Are you sorry about it?"

I knew what she meant.

"No!"

I moved over beside Kathleen and kissed her. Tweaked a handy nipple under her t-shirt. Palmed her breast.

"How about you?"

Kathleen smiled. Extended her hand to rub me for a moment.

"No, I'm not sorry. I'm satisfied, I guess, if that makes any sense. I don't think Chloe is sorry, either."

She looked out the window at our soggy and bedraggled garden.

"I don't know whether it'll ever happen again. Doesn't matter. It's what Chloe wants, not us."

Another pause. Another long look out the window. When Kathleen turned back she was smiling.

"I dunno. I really don't. But I'm betting our daughter has something up her sleeve. And I think I'm going to like it."

Another pause. She grinned.

"If I'm right, you're going to like it, too."

I stood and pulled Kathleen to me. I kissed her, thoroughly, rubbing my hands up and down her back as she molded herself against me and purred into my mouth ...

Afterwards, I gently disengaged from Kathleen and got the

throw we keep on the back of the sofa. The gas fire was warm but with the rain and cold outside it was still too cool without a coverup.

Kathleen smiled.

"Mmm. That was nice."

I hugged her and kissed her.

"I think we'd better get dressed before Chloe comes back, no?"

Her breasts lifted as Kathleen shoved the throw away and rolled onto her back and stretched her arms above her head, her parted thighs an invitation I forced myself to ignore.

"Spoilsport."

I grilled steaks that night. We keep the Weber right outside on the covered patio and I never let a little rain discourage me. Chloe was back by the time I had the fire started. I seasoned the steaks while Chloe and her mother worked up a green salad.

I'd be kidding if I said I wasn't a little on edge. Pictures? I'm a voyeur at heart, I admit it, and it hadn't escaped my memory that what set off things in our household last fall was an image of Chloe in her dusky rose underwear, even if I learned later the underwear was actually a swimsuit.

By the time we'd finished dinner and washed up I was more than on edge, I was flat-out horny. I didn't know what Chloe had in mind—beyond the pictures, that is—but I had my hopes. Even if they didn't work out exactly that way, I thought to myself, Kathleen was here.

"OK, guys, here we go."

Chloe, seated between us, opened her laptop on the coffee table.

"It's a slideshow. I'm going to start it and let it run, OK?"

Kathleen and I nodded. I put my arm around Chloe's shoulders and she snuggled against me.

The first image set the tone. It was Chloe in her bikini, smiling at the camera, the hillside behind her as green as California hills get as soon as the rains start, the sunlight slanting late in the afternoon and outlining the red tiles on the buildings seen in the distance behind her.

The next few images showed Chloe posing, cheesecake-style, hips canted, mugging and pouting for the camera. In one or two Robert appeared, bare-chested in what looked like board shorts, his swimmer's, we learned later, form showing to advantage as he matched Chloe's poses.

Chloe's bare breasts changed the mood fast. Gone were the smirks and funny faces. Her curves were golden in the afternoon light. There was warmth in her eyes and love, too, in the way she looked straight into the lens.

I stirred, shifted in my seat, and tightened my arm around Chloe's shoulders. She turned and kissed my cheek. She followed up with Kathleen a moment later. I thought I saw them kiss on the lips, but I'm not sure.

On the screen, Chloe was stretched on the grass, nude now, relaxed and open. Inviting. What or whom was she inviting?

I wondered how far these images would go, and got my answer when the show ended with Chloe on her tummy, her firm bottom centered in the screen, the camera following the curves of her back, smooth top to bottom, her head turned enough for us to see her smile.

Beside me, Chloe stirred. Turned slightly, her breast pressing my side, smiling but with a question in her eyes.

I had to stop a moment to catch my breath. Kissed her on the lips, lightly.

"Lovely, sweetie."

Chloe smiled.

"There's more, but maybe I should stop here?"

"OK, Chloe."

I heard Kathleen's disappointment. I cleared my throat and

hoped I didn't sound the same.

"Chloe, tell us about Rob, OK?"

Chloe smiled.

"I like him. I guess that's obvious, huh?"

She paused.

"We were in the same Western Civ section last quarter. That's where we met. Kind of funny. I knew who he was, of course. It's a small section. One day we ended up sitting beside each other. Until that day, we'd done nothing more than nod to each other, and his voice startled me a little.

" 'So, what did you think of Hollister?'

"I turned to look at this tall guy beside me. Kind of cute, I already knew that. Half-smile.

" 'Boring.'

"He laughed.

" 'You got that right.'

"He stuck out his hand.

" 'Rob.'

" 'Chloe.'

"We shook. Very formal, huh? Every couple of weeks we get a lecture from some big shot expert. Hollister was supposed to know everything about 'Church and State in the Middle Ages.' Yeah, right. There was no way to tell what he knew. Maybe if he used an outline it would help. I'm an ace notetaker, but I couldn't follow Hollister's presentation to save my life.

" 'How about Jameson's lecture a couple of weeks ago?'

"I wasn't listening. Dreamy. There's no other word for it. Rob was dreamy. Is dreamy. My tummy did a little flutter."

Chloe turned to Kathleen and began to stroke her cheek and neck with the tips of her fingers. I could almost hear Kathleen's purr behind her smile.

"Anyway, it took me a second to come back to earth.

" 'What?'

" 'Renaissance Art. Two weeks ago, remember?'

" 'Oh, yeah. Good. It was really good.'

"I guess it was good. I was too lost in Rob's brown eyes to know what I was saying. Or care.

" 'Want to go for coffee?'

"Yes, I did. I felt a tingle and squished it. Stop it, you fool, I thought to myself. It's just coffee. Get a grip. Keep your pants on."

Chloe interrupted her stroking of Kathleen and leaned over to kiss Kathleen's cheek, her neck.

"Trouble was, I was having trouble with that. Getting a grip, I mean. I jumped when I felt Rob's hand on my arm.

" 'You OK?'

"I covered his hand with my own.

" 'Yeah! Let's go.' "

Chloe kissed Kathleen again. Giggled.

"Anyway, that's how we met!"

I shifted and began to stroke the back of Chloe's neck. Moved a little to run my fingers under her ear and down the side and back again. Chloe's turn to purr.

Chloe stood up, stretched like a cat. A curvy cat. She had our attention, but I was kind of frustrated when she leaned down to kiss Kathleen, then me, lightly on the lips and announced she was off to bed.

"Maybe I'll tell you more tomorrow morning, OK?"

I forced a smile. Jesus, was this kid ever playing me. Us.

"Sure, Chloe."

Chloe was on hands and knees, her rump in the air, smooth, inviting. Someone behind her, his face obscured, his hips jack-hammering Chloe, her breasts swaying with every thrust.

Chloe couldn't speak because she'd wrapped her lips around someone else's thick cock, the thrusts of her lover behind her forcing the cock in front deeper and deeper into her throat. The movements behind her grew more frantic, even as the cock in front increased its thrusts, hands holding her head steady, her tongue briefly glimpsed under said cock.

It was all over in a moment. The cock in front spurted and she swallowed again and again. Behind her, the guy never let go of her hips while he released and delivered.

I opened my eyes when I felt soft paws on my chest. Large cat, yellow eyes two inches from mine. George, of course, reminding me he was ready for his morning treat.

This morning, though, my treat came first. Kathleen stirred as I dislodged George and rolled over on top of Kathleen, fitting myself between her butt cheeks. Paused for a moment to pull my boxers down and free my cock. Stroked and thrust along the outside of her panties, her soft warmth yielding as I ground against her. She groaned as I pulled her t-shirt up and reached under her to cup and press her tits, her nipples hard and welcoming my touch. I was already more than halfway there after my Chloe dream, and I erupted after only a half-dozen strokes and covered her smooth back.

Kathleen lay quiet for a few moments, then wriggled her bottom to signal it was time. Her smile belied the sleepiness in her eyes.

"My turn."

I whipped off my t-shirt and cleaned Kathleen's back before she moved. When she turned over I skinned her panties down and off and dove into her warm humid muskiness and let my tongue do the talking.

"Love you."

"Love you."

My cheeks were wet with her juices as I moved up her torso and kissed her, morning breath and all.

"Hi guys!"

Chloe joined us for coffee at the kitchen table.

"So, what did you think?"

I looked at Kathleen.

"Chloe, you both looked great."

Kathleen paused. Grinned.

"Hot, too. Both of you."

Chloe laughed and jumped up to hug Kathleen first, then me.

"Thanks, Mom, thanks, Dad.

"There's more to show you, but they get pretty, um, personal, you know?"

I hoped she couldn't see my erection under the table. I reached over to take her hand.

"Can't wait, Chloe."

She laughed again.

"Great! Tonight, OK? Gotta go. Bye Mom, bye Dad."

Kathleen and I were left looking at each other. I jumped up to grab Kathleen, going for a repeat of our earlier romp, but she stopped me with her hand out.

"Easy, tiger. Why don't we see what happens tonight?"

She leaned her face up for a kiss.

"No matter what happens, you and I are going to get lucky. That's a promise."

Her lips confirmed it.

Kathleen made her famous minestrone for dinner. That and a bottle of middling red, plus a sweet bâtard from our favorite bakery, Spanish-speakers all but boy can they ever bake French, hit the spot on this cold evening with the rain a never-ending drizzle and a ground fog rising outside.

Chloe did the dishes while Kathleen and I showered and put on comfy fireside sweats and t-shirts. After she finished in the kitchen Chloe did the same, and we reconvened in the living room with the rest of the wine and hot coffee in a vacuum container for later. I was hoping there would be a "later," at any rate.

"So, I found out Rob's a swimmer, too. Not team-level like I am, but good enough that we started doing laps together after I ran into him at the Aquatic Center one afternoon. He looks good in a Speedo, really good."

Chloe stroked Kathleen's hair as she spoke.

"Anyway, we got into the habit of getting a coffee after swimming. Later on we started studying together."

Chloe giggled.

"And, well, one thing led to another, as you saw last night."

She paused.

"Are you guys sure you want to see this? Some of the images are really strong, you know?"

Kathleen and I sandwiched Chloe with a hug. I stroked her cheek.

"Sweetie, whatever you want to show us, we'd like to see."

Kathleen echoed me.

Chloe gave us each a kiss.

"OK. Don't say I didn't warn you."

We settled in, Chloe snuggled between us, as her images began to display. The scene shifted to what I recognized as Sylvia's family cabin, easily identified by those moose heads we'd seen first at Thanksgiving last year. A fire in the fireplace, Chloe and Sylvia stretched out in front on their tummies to start. I'm not sure I can remember all of the images, much less describe them, but it was quite clear the two girls and Ryan enjoyed themselves as Rob documented every wriggle and spasm and throb.

The last sequence ended with a smiling Sylvia sandwiched between Chloe and Ryan.

After the last image I stretched, and scratched Chloe lightly on the back of her neck. Kathleen spoke first.

"Well, Chloe."

Kathleen stopped.

"Mom?"

"I think your mother means, 'Wow,' sweetie."

Chloe squeezed Kathleen, kissed her. She turned to me and repeated her squeeze and kiss.

"Mom, Dad, there's more."

"Oh?"

"Yeah. Ryan did a little film with Rob's camera, too."

"Let's see."

Double wow.

I don't know that Rob was the biggest guy I'd ever seen, but he sure as hell knew how to use what he had. Not just what he was packing between his legs, but his tongue and his mouth and his hands as well. He had Chloe up, down and sideways and if her grimaces and cries and laughs were any indication she enjoyed every second of it. I'll even give him extra points for something else—instead of the usual flashy finish he remained solidly implanted in Chloe, her legs tight around his butt, as he spasmed and squirmed against her.

The scene ended when Sylvia, who had been stroking Chloe whenever and wherever she could, got to her feet and sashayed up to the camera, her boobs filling the screen until the view shifted and the camera came to rest on its side on the sofa and we watched Sylvia ride Ryan, hard.

"Um, Mom, Dad?"

We looked at Chloe.

"There's something else."

Kathleen stroked Chloe's hair.

"What, sweetie?"

"It's about Rob."

Christ, I was thinking, what else could there be?

"He likes to experiment."

Kathleen glanced at me as she continued to stroke Chloe's hair.

"Like what, Chloe?"

Chloe twisted to kiss her mother, and back to kiss me, this time on the lips, and she lingered.

"Like with guys."

I felt my cock twitch. I was thinking about our last conversation a few weeks ago with our friend Malcolm and his new love, a guy.

"There's another film, but I promised I wouldn't show it to you unless they said it was OK."

"Who, Chloe?"

"Rob. And, um, Ryan."

Now I was seriously hard. I hadn't even met Rob yet but there were some possibilities here.

Chloe smiled.

"I just thought you guys should know."

Kathleen beat me to it.

"Sweetie, if they say it's OK, we'd like to see that film, too."

"Yeah."

That's about all I could manage.

Chloe's smile got broader.

"I think you guys will like it."

She paused. Turned to me and kissed my mouth, a little harder this time.

"Especially you, Dad."

We were quiet for a couple of moments until Chloe rose from the couch and extended her arms over her head in a luxurious stretch. That ended with a yelp as Kathleen and I attacked from opposite sides. Her laughter and giggles became groans and murmurs when Kathleen lifted Chloe's t-shirt off and we each began to nuzzle and nip at Chloe's breasts. Chloe turned to Kathleen to hold her head and kiss Kathleen full on the lips. I followed Chloe's twist and in a moment I was cupping and palming Chloe's breasts from behind. I turned a little more and pulled Chloe down on top of me, Kathleen following, and we ended up in a squirming pile on the couch.

Sure, we attacked her, no warning, but I knew we'd been set up and Chloe's struggles seemed to be mostly aimed at getting herself out of her clothes as fast as she could. Kathleen and I took care of our own, and in a moment we were on the rug in front of the fire and we had Chloe sandwiched nicely between us and we were kissing every single inch of her.

Our sandwich fell apart as Chloe shifted to part Kathleen's thighs and move to her center where Chloe's tongue found warm and wet places to conquer. That was fine with me. I moved on my knees closer to Chloe's bottom, held her by the hips and sank into her. Chloe stopped what she was doing with Kathleen for a second and looked back at me, and I understood her smoky expression perfectly.

I jackhammered Chloe and I didn't last long, but that was OK because a little later we switched around and before the evening was over I'd come again, this time on Kathleen's boobs, and I'd tasted both women to loud happy climaxes.

Chloe returned to school a couple of days later, and in a week or so she sent us a link to her Cloud storage site.

The short clip didn't need to be any longer than it was, considering it ended with Rob coming all over Ryan's face while Chloe rubbed Rob's butt and Sylvia held Ryan from behind and stroked his erect cock and both girls laughed and laughed. I think Ryan's cum-covered smile was genuine, and Rob looked pretty pleased with himself.

It left me with a hard-on, to Kathleen's amusement.

"OK, pal, is this what I think it is?"

She kept stroking.

"He's pretty good-looking, you know?"

"Yeah, buddy, I know. You apparently like more than his looks, right?"

I was close.

"Oh, man."

"Come on me, John."

I did.

Later, after I returned the favor, we rested in each other's arms.

"John, are you thinking about Malcolm?"

I stirred.

"And his new love. And that weekend with Susan and Victoria."

Kathleen squeezed me.

"Me, too."

As it turned out, the weekend several years ago we spent at the clothing-optional resort with Malcolm and Susan and their younger daughter, Victoria, was the last time we saw Susan. A month later, Malcolm told us she'd been diagnosed with an inoperable brain tumor. Six months after that she was dead.

Last year we'd gone hiking with Malcolm. At lunch afterwards, he told us he had something he wanted to share. You could have knocked us over with a feather when he said he'd developed a relationship with a man, someone he'd met through a music class he was taking. When I asked him what kind of relationship, his answer was, "A full one."

Pressed about what this meant for his marriage to Susan, he laughed and said that was exactly the question Victoria and Mercedes, his older girl, had asked. It resulted in several very awkward conversations with his daughters, he told us, the upshot of which was that he'd loved Susan completely, no regrets, no hesitations or conditions, and this new relationship had simply happened on its own. No labels, only that at least right now he was in a full relationship with a man.

I asked him what it was like when he and I had coffee a couple of weeks later. I confess I was interested in the details. I'd done the fooling around when I was a teenager that a lot of guys do, even if they don't talk about it, and what Malcolm told me increased my interest. Christ, that's a stupid way to put it. It turned me on, some of it. I'm afraid the full penetration part didn't interest me, but the stroking and the rubbing and the mouth work sure did.

It reminded me of the fooling around with others Kathleen and I had done ourselves, in college and later, including that Caribbean holiday Kathleen told Chloe about at Christmas. We'd sure done more than skinnydipping with Jill and Ed Robinson. There was one warm evening when, after an extended session, each with the other's wife, Jill and I were lying together when I felt someone lightly stroking my back from my neck all the way down to my rear end. It was relaxing and exciting at the same time. The breeze through our open windows was cool on my skin, and after a few minutes the stroking was starting to arouse me once more. When I felt myself stiffening I kissed Jill and turned onto my back, expecting to see Kathleen. It was Ed. For a second, only a second, I was about to object, until I heard a stifled giggle behind me, and at the same time saw Kathleen grinning behind and to the side of Ed.

"Ed?"

"Relax, buddy. You're going to like this."

I was getting seriously hard after Ed dropped his hand to my cock and began stroking in earnest. Kathleen nodded when I looked her way, she knew me, she knew this wasn't the first time a guy had had his hands on me, so I followed Ed's advice and relaxed. Ed dropped his head to my lap and took me inside, his lips and tongue as warm and wet as any other I'd experienced.

He sucked, he cradled my balls, he kissed me and licked me and that was it. I came pretty hard considering I'd been with Jill only a little while earlier.

It took me a few minutes to get my breath back, Ed sitting there, big smile on his face. I knew I'd been set up when the women high-fived each other. Ed and I looked at each other. I'd been wondering whether Ed wanted me to return the favor and I was very interested in doing that if only to get back at him, but the women congratulating each other could not be let to stand without retaliation. So I grabbed Kathleen, Ed did the same with Jill, and as they squirmed frantically we first kissed and sucked and then ate them into submission. Ed had pinned Jill to the floor with his cock, her legs back against her boobs, and he did his best to fuck her silly. By some miracle after a few more minutes I was hard enough, so I emulated Ed's efforts and screwed Kathleen to within an inch of her life. That sounds terrible, except it was exactly what the women wanted and we knew it. Afterwards, the two lay there totally flattened and it was our turn to high-five each other.

I was interested in playing with Rob or at least seeing what might happen, Kathleen knew it, so I sent Chloe a little note. "Sweetie, you were right. We're going to enjoy meeting Rob, me especially." I laughed when I showed Chloe's reply to Kathleen. "Me, too!"

Later that night, after I'd eaten Kathleen until she pushed me away, laughing, and she'd returned the favor and we were lying side-by-side, I heard Kathleen giggle.

"What?"

She laughed.

"Are you going to tell Chloe about that afternoon in the meadow?"

Christ. Not that I'd forgotten that. It was B.C., Before Chloe, and A.C., After College, but we were all still in our twenties, all starting out in our careers, and we were palling around with a mixed bunch, not everyone paired off but all of us pretty good buddies.

"Think I should?"

She poked me.

"Why not?"

Remembering that afternoon, I felt my cock stirring, not that anything was really going to happen right now.

"We were high, right?"

"You don't remember?"

Oh no, I remembered everything. The warm afternoon, the soft grass under us, not to mention the grass we were smoking. There was a beer or five, too. We were high and wired. There'd been other afternoons, maybe not quite the same combination of people, where things had gotten loose, really loose.

Kathleen started to stroke me.

"Remember who stripped first?"

I did.

"Oh, yeah. Veronica, of course."

Kathleen's friend, Veronica. Veronica was always the first. Anyway, one thing led to another, and before long we were all nude. There was some dancing, I remember, and some kissing. Lots of kissing. Lots. People seemed to coalesce in pairs, in threesomes. I remember Clive on top of me, rubbing his erection along mine, Kathleen beside us. And, well, things went on from there. I think we all got off, and mine wasn't the only cock in another guy's mouth that afternoon. Don't get the wrong idea, it wasn't all guy-on-guy. Clive helped me sandwich Emily a little later, and I had Kathleen as well all by myself before the afternoon was over.

Kathleen hugged me and stroked me and that was all I remembered that night.

Unfortunately, a winter flu meant we had to scrap our plans for a February weekend with Chloe and Rob, to our mutual disappointment. Mine, especially, considering what I'd seen in Chloe's last movie. So, we didn't see either of them except for an extended Skype session after they recovered. Rob seemed to be very interested in what we thought of the movie.

Kathleen answered, looking first at me, then at the screen.

"It was totally hot, and you should have seen him!"

I think Kathleen's laughter and her poke in my ribs reassured Rob. I saw Chloe relax at that, too, and she and Rob exchanged a quick look.

Chloe waved at the screen.

"You're on! Bye!"

Kathleen turned to me after we signed off.

"John, I'd like to see Chloe and Rob at Easter. What do you think?"

A no-brainer.

"You bet. What about Ryan and Sylvia?"

"Sure, if Chloe wants to invite them."

I was thinking about fun with Ryan, too.

Spring came early with a string of warm days and very cool nights, so two weeks before Easter we took the cover off and cleaned the pool. After we launched our pool season privately in our usual fashion, Kathleen and I stretched out on the grass, still nude and a little sweaty, our fingers lightly linked.

"So, John, plans for Rob?"

Yes, I was thinking.

"Maybe."

"Good."

I didn't have to ask. I knew she had plans for Rob, too.

The kids, minus Ryan, arrived in a happy laughing bunch around noon on Good Friday, in the middle of what the weather twits said was going to be a week-long spell of unseasonably warm days. Rob in the flesh proved to be as attractive as he'd been on the screen. Kathleen prolonged her welcome by enough to signal Rob she really was glad to see him. I liked his smile and firm handshake.

Kathleen looked around.

"Where's Ryan, Chloe?"

Sylvia broke in.

"Chicago."

We must have looked blank.

"His uncle is ill, and his folks wanted everyone to visit now rather than later."

Sylvia turned to Kathleen, grinned.

"He's really going to miss this visit."

Her grin got wider.

"Really."

Kathleen blushed. I knew she was thinking about Christmas at Lake Tahoe.

"Which means," Sylvia added, looking at me, "you and Rob are going to be busy."

I glanced at Rob, who shrugged and smiled. Kathleen stepped into the pause.

"The guest room is made up."

She looked from one to the other.

"Or you can camp out in the living room, if you like."

"OK, Mom. No worries. We'll figure it out."

With that, Chloe led them off to dump their stuff and change into swimsuits.

I looked at Kathleen.

"Join them?"

Kathleen shrugged.

"In a little while. Let them have some time by themselves."

"OK."

We made it out to the pool about a half-hour later, to discover that they'd all dispensed with bathing suits and were lined up in a row sunning, Rob in the middle on his back. Chloe gave us a little wave. Sylvia looked to be dozing, her bottom as inviting as ever. To judge by his lazy erection and half-embarrassed smile and Chloe's grin, Rob had been enjoying a little mild dalliance with Chloe.

Kathleen stripped off her suit, smiling at Chloe and Rob.

"Don't let us interrupt, kids."

I tried to look nonchalant and harmless, but probably my own semi-hardness said something else when I stepped out of my own trunks. As a distraction I grabbed Kathleen and shoved her into the pool and jumped in behind her. She sputtered for a moment but I silenced her by kissing her. Her sputters changed to grunts of approval as she wrapped her legs around me and rubbed herself against my now totally erect cock. I let her go on for a moment before I released her and swam to the deep end of the pool. Kathleen followed, and a moment later I felt her hand on my erection.

"Is this for me, or someone else?"

"Always for you, sweetie, but at the moment, well, um?"

She giggled.

"It's Rob, isn't it?"

I think I blushed.

"Well, only if he's interested."

We heard splashes.

Kathleen looked to the shallow end, where Rob and Chloe were entwined, Chloe imitating her mother's movements from earlier.

"Why don't we find out?"

By the time we got to the shallow end Rob had boosted Chloe onto the deck and buried his face between her thighs, her legs on his shoulders. All to Chloe's delight, it was obvious, her eyes closed, her tummy undulating, and a big grin plastered across her face.

Feeling bold, I moved up behind Rob and rubbed his rear end. He wriggled in response. Kathleen's hand replaced mine, and I levered myself out of the shallow end and headed for the grass where Sylvia, her hand between her legs, needed assistance. I assisted her.

When I caught my breath, and after a long set of post-coital, "Hi, how are you," kisses, I sat up to see how the other three were doing. There was no cause for concern. Kathleen and Chloe were seated side-by-side, their hands all over each other as Rob's tongue alternated between them, and I wondered which one he was going to have first. I got my answer when instead of taking one or both of them Rob came up the steps and over to Sylvia and slipped his cock into her waiting mouth. I guess they'd practiced this. After a couple of minutes he withdrew and turned to me, and I wondered whose mouth he was going to put that thing in next. But Rob only smiled, jacked himself twice, and covered Sylvia's pretty face.

I was fiddling with the grill later that afternoon when I heard Rob behind me.

"Mr. Davidson?"

I turned around. I wondered for a second whether to insist on the formality or let him off the hook.

"Hey, Rob. It's John. What's up?"

Rob looked a little uncertain for a moment.

"Well, I wanted you to know, I mean to ask, um, about Chloe?"

I waited. Figured the kid needed to speak for himself.

"I mean, are you and Mrs. Davidson OK with me and Chloe?"

"Rob, Chloe's told us how she feels about you, which means you're OK with us."

I grinned.

"Besides, we've seen the movie, remember?"

That relieved Rob, I could see that. I put him to work making burger patties while we talked. Every dad worries about his daughter and there's always a little bit of possessiveness with another male. Might sound odd, considering our family relationship, but there it was.

On the other hand, the more I listened to Rob talk about school, swimming, and the other stuff he and Chloe and their gang were up to this quarter, the more impressed I was. The kid was smart, funny, and warm without trying to grease me up. Or if he was greasing me up he was so good at it I didn't notice.

Later that evening, stuffed on burgers, we were all in the living room, Kathleen and me on the sofa, Rob in the corner easy chair, and the girls in front of the fire. Kathleen asked the question I was wondering about.

"Rob, Chloe says your family is in New Mexico?"

"Yeah. Mom, Dad, and my little sister. She's in high school still. Dad's an architect and my mom's a psychologist. She has a home office that's private and her clients come to her. Casey's a swimmer, like me."

Kathleen looked at me, raised her eyebrows. I nodded. I was about to ask the thing on my mind when Chloe sat up and turned around.

"I know what you're going to ask, Dad."

She turned to Rob.

"Go ahead and tell them, sweetie. It's OK."

Rob looked a little uncertain. Chloe smiled.

"Really, Rob, it's OK."

"My family is really close."

Well, this was interesting. Rob paused for a moment, I guess to decide what to say next.

"I mean, maybe not as close as you all are, but close."

Chloe moved over to sit in front of him between his knees. Rob started massaging her shoulders.

"We also spend a lot of time nude."

Hmm.

"I mean, just nude. My sister and I haven't done anything, really. A little kissing a few years ago when she started to get boobs and all. A little rubbing, too, to make each other feel good."

He kept working on Chloe's shoulders. Happy sigh from Chloe.

"Then we found out about our parents. We didn't spy on them or anything. They told us straight out. My sister and I didn't really know what to think. It wasn't like Mom and Dad were inviting us to share or play with them. They weren't, but they told us we could watch if we wanted to, as long as we stayed out of sight."

Rob slipped his hands down Chloe's front and cradled her breasts. I put my arm around Kathleen and hugged her.

"So we did. That night we almost had sex, too, but we stopped at the last minute. I'm not sure why, because watching my dad take Mrs. Smith from next door from behind was almost too much. And when Mr. Nelson from down the block came all over Mom's boobs, my sister groaned and came without me even touching her. That was it for me and I spurted all over the carpet."

Rob let go of Chloe's boobs and returned to her shoulders. Chloe frowned. Sylvia, who was watching, giggled.

"That's about it, I guess."

Rob looked from one to the other of us. Kathleen sat up and walked over to Rob, leaned past Chloe and kissed him. She turned to me.

"Let's go, pal."

She turned back as we headed down the hall.

"Enjoy yourselves, kids."

We'd barely stripped and gotten settled in bed when Kathleen turned to me and put her hand on my chest.

"Shall we go see, maybe in a little while?"

"Sure."

There's a place where you can see the fire and the carpet in front of it from the hall and not be noticed if you're quiet and the hall is dark. That night we could see just fine.

Chloe and Sylvia, nude now, were locked in a kiss, their legs intertwined and scissoring, hands finding good places to pet and stroke and rub. Rob was nearby, stroking himself slowly but not touching either girl. As he watched, Chloe reached her climax, shuddering, little cries escaping from her kiss with Sylvia. I don't know how close Sylvia was, but instead of continuing she released Chloe and turned onto her back in front of Rob.

"On me, Rob."

Her voice was low and urgent. Rob moved closer to Sylvia and speeded up. Sylvia had one hand on her right breast and the other moving quickly between her legs.

"Go, sweetie!"

Rob spurted on her tummy and hand. Chloe watched, leaning on one elbow, until Rob sank to his knees, holding his softening cock. Rob stretched out beside Chloe and she held him in her arms.

We stepped back, silently, and closed our bedroom door quietly. Kathleen took me, rigid and trembling, in her mouth. When I came, she swallowed it all and nursed me, her tongue barely moving, as I shrank. When she came back from brushing her teeth, she refused my offer to return the favor.

"I'm sleepy. Hold me."

She pressed her bottom against me and I held her boob gently while we spooned. Kathleen yawned, a real jaw-cracker.

"Rob. I like him."

"Me, too," I responded, but I think Kathleen was already asleep.

Saturday morning I was up early. Kathleen opened her eyes and gave me a little wave as I got up to make coffee. When I turned back at the door I saw she'd closed her eyes and gone back to sleep. I was up early, but when I got to the living room it was apparent that the kids had gotten up even earlier. Chloe was stretched out on her tummy, her midsection raised on one of the sofa cushions far enough for Rob to enter her from behind, his hands holding her buttocks, his thrusts moving her forward. Sylvia smiled when she saw me, but Chloe and Rob were too much in their own moment to notice.

I was filling the kettle at the kitchen sink when a warm body pressed against me and a hand came around to stroke my now-erect cock.

"Good morning, John."

I could hear the smile in Sylvia's voice. I turned around and held her, warm and smooth and equally nude, in my arms. I kissed her and ran my hands over her bottom. Pulled back to see the laughter in her eyes. The challenge, too.

I was more than ready, so I cupped her breasts briefly, turned her, and bent her over the kitchen table. She was wet and ready, and she groaned with pleasure as I sank into her. I held her hips and hammered her, not caring about anything other than fucking her as hard and as fast as I could. She was primed and her cries and grunts stoked my fires when she peaked, happily before I did, although at that point I didn't really care whether she did or not, and a moment later I jammed myself as far inside her as I could, pulling her hard against me, and I spasmed and filled her.

"Yeah, Dad!"

I withdrew from Sylvia and turned to see Chloe in the doorway, Rob behind her, his hands on her hips. I helped Sylvia straighten up, kissed her, and grabbed a dish towel for her to use to clean up. As I stepped past Chloe I kissed her, and touched Rob lightly on the arm.

Back in our bedroom I found Kathleen awake and bright-eyed, and I put my head between her thighs and inhaled her fragrance and made her come and come with my lips and tongue and fingers until she pushed me away. I crawled up let her taste herself when I kissed her. Lying half on top of her I heard her giggle.

"Well, I guess the kids are up, huh?"

I laughed.

"Oh, yeah."

I kissed Kathleen again, lingering a little this time.

"Rob made Chloe really happy."

Before I could continue Kathleen reached for me. I was still a little sticky from earlier, I guess, and she noticed.

"And you and Sylvia?"

"I bent her over the kitchen table and fucked her."

"How romantic, John."

"She wasn't in the mood for romance."

I knew it was going to happen. I wanted it to happen. It was inevitable, really. By Saturday afternoon it had warmed up even a little more than the day before. That wasn't entirely good news, because the forecast now said there was a good chance of rain overnight and maybe on Easter morning, too. We'd been to our favorite grocery store that morning after breakfast, and Kathleen had our butterflied leg of lamb marinating for tomorrow.

We were out at the pool again, no swimsuits, sunbathing in a row and Kathleen was putting sunblock on Rob while Chloe did the same for Sylvia. Kathleen had already done me, my back, and I was dozing when I heard Kathleen whispering to Rob. I couldn't hear the words, but I did hear Rob chuckle.

"OK, John, you take over."

Kathleen handed me the container of sunblock. I looked at her, at Rob. Christ, I thought to myself. Who am I kidding, anyway? The moment was here. The one underlying this whole weekend, and everyone knew it.

I took the container and swung my leg over Rob's butt and began to work on his back, my cock finding something it liked and growing. After a few strokes I gave up pretending and tossed the container aside. Raised my hips a little and straightened my cock and slid it along Rob's crease, the lotion making us nice and slippery.

"OK, Rob?"

He wriggled beneath me, and that was answer enough for me. I rubbed myself on his rear end, faster as I got closer. Rob pressed back a little, and Kathleen hovered beside me and kissed me. I sprayed Bob's back with what felt like a gallon of cum. I was quiet for a moment, and lifted off when Rob pushed up at me.

I knew what was coming next and I wasn't disappointed as Rob got to his knees, his cock stiff. I bent down and took him, firm and round and smooth, into my mouth, sucked him and licked him and at the end held still as Rob fucked my face, hard. At the very last moment he pulled out and came all over Kathleen right beside me.

Sylvia and Chloe clapped.

It rained overnight, and Sunday morning brought a fog and light drizzle. Sunrise was at 7:00 a.m. this year, well, 6:57 a.m. to be exact, but fortunately our church's service was held in a meadow only a few miles away, so we were up early enough and had a bit of fruit and coffee to hold us. The rain slacked off to a heavy mist when we arrived in the parking lot below the meadow, and a few hundred wet yards later we were there. No sunrise, but the metaphor was not lost.

Pastor Bob kept things short, probably to the dismay of those few traditionalists in our relatively liberal congregation, but the service was as long as it needed to be and not a minute longer, to my relief. Afterwards, we devoured pancakes and bacon and lots of hot coffee afterwards at our local IHOP, still early enough to beat the post-Easter-service crowd. The kids chowed down like they hadn't eaten for days.

By noon the sky cleared and it was warming again, and by mid-afternoon I had the fire going and the lamb grilling, with an inviting aroma from the marinade. We feasted.

Late Sunday evening found us inside once more in front of the fire, all quiet. Myself, I had reached that level of contentment good food and good company bring and I was coasting, enjoying the moment. Slowly the hugs and strokes and kisses became more intense. All very gradual, but I began to stiffen as I watched Chloe and Sylvia embrace, moving against each other, their thighs intertwined. I heard a rustle as Rob mounted Kathleen, her breasts quivering as he began thrusting, their mouths locked together. As they moved faster, I put my wine down and moved closer. Rob glanced at me, smiled, turned his attention once more to Kathleen, and continued doing his best to drive her into the carpet.

Watching Kathleen, I decided she wasn't going to get off easily. My chance came when Rob thrust once more and remained still as he emptied himself inside her. In a moment or two he withdrew to Kathleen's side. Kathleen turned to me, and in a second I was inside her humping to beat the band. I didn't give a thought to whether she was enjoying this, I didn't care at all. I only wanted to fuck her and fuck her and blast inside her. I got my wish.

At last Kathleen and I struggled to our feet.

"Goodnight, kids."

"Wait!"

Chloe kissed Sylvia and Rob, lingering a little with Rob, and got up to follow us.

"I'm sleeping with you guys tonight."

Monday morning came early and so did I, Chloe too, me inside her, her thighs holding me tight and my hands on her boobs. I watched Chloe come again a little while later as Kathleen ate her.

"Thanks, Dad!"

Chloe's cheek was soft against mine, her lips warm, and I hugged her and squeezed her and didn't want to let her go, ever.

"I love you, Chloe."

"I love you, Dad."

She kissed me once more and moved to Kathleen to repeat her farewell.

I shook Rob's hand and looked him in the eye and smiled. That's all we needed to do. A hug and kiss for Sylvia, and the three of them were on their way.

I had my arm around Kathleen's waist as we watched them pull out. I turned Kathleen to me and kissed her.

"Happy Easter, Kathleen."

"Happy Easter, sweetie."

Printed in Great Britain
by Amazon